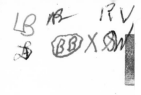

RENEGADE CANYON

Also by Peter Dawson
in Thorndike Large Print ®

Gunsmoke Graze
Royal Gorge
High Country
Big Outfit

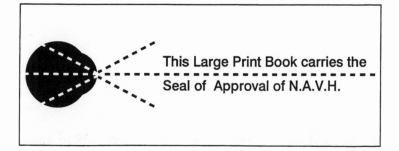

This Large Print Book carries the
Seal of Approval of N.A.V.H.

RENEGADE CANYON

13-10-1128

PETER DAWSON

Thorndike Press • Thorndike, Maine

Thorndike Large Print® Western Series.

Published in 1993 by arrangement with Golden West Literary Agency.

The tree indicium is a trademark of Thorndike Press.

The text of this Large Print edition is unabridged. Other aspects of the book may vary from the original.

Set 16 pt. News Plantin by Barbara Ingerson.

Printed in the United States on acid-free, high opacity paper.∞

Library of Congress Cataloging in Publication Data

Dawson, Peter, 1907–
    Renegade Canyon / by Peter Dawson.
      p.   cm.
    ISBN 1-56054-704-9 (alk. paper : lg. print)
    1. Large type books. I. Title.
  [PS3507.A848R46   1993]
  813'.54—dc 20   93-35501

RENEGADE
CANYON

Chapter One

Toward eleven that morning he had several fleeting glimpses of the formation assembling, though the guard-house window let him see only the far edge of the log-palisaded parade so that he couldn't be exactly sure of what was going on. There was one moment's keen lift of pride that crowded out his deep depression as K Troop trotted smartly across his narrow field of vision. Afterward he ran a hand over his dark hair, then along his flat, clean-shaven cheeks, and finally down to smooth his dark blue tunic, the gestures automatic and prompted by the unconscious wish that there should be no flaw in his appearance.

At the approach of this critical moment for which he had been waiting these many interminable days, Dan Gentry found himself drained of all emotion. That was in a way surprising, for at this turning-point in his life he had supposed he would be plagued by bitterness and regret. But both were long gone, buried deep under the weight of four weeks' solitary reflection that had added up to nothing but a complete and confounding failure at un-

7

derstanding why this should be happening to him.

Nothing remained but to undergo the unpleasantness of the ceremony that would punctuate the already established facts. He was wishing only that this was over, that he could finally be away from here and on his own.

The abrupt and heavy thud of boots along the corridor planking turned him from the barred window now, and in the gloom beyond the cell grating he made out two figures approaching. The taller was oppressively familiar. But sight of the other, short, stocky, and with a saber under arm, stirred in him a pleasurable anticipation he managed to conceal nicely as the padlock was rattling against the hasp.

"That'll be all, Corporal."

Sergeant Tim McCune spoke brittlely and waited out there watching the tall trooper go back along the corridor. Only at the hollow slam of the guardroom door did his glance swing around to Gentry. He stepped into the cell then, drew stiffly to attention, and saluted.

Gentry returned the salute and over an interval of several seconds the two eyed each other silently. The way McCune's round Irish face slowly lost its enigmatic set before a tightening expression of naked despair finally made Gentry drawl, "Well, Sergeant, it'll all be over half an hour from now."

"So it will, sir." McCune shook his head in a baffled way. There was a pleading for understanding in his glance as he went on. "Captain, you told me not to, but I've been watchin' him. Every minute off duty. Last night I was there in his barn-loft keepin' an eye on that shack where he sleeps. It was like all the other times. There's been nothing, not one damned thing, to tie him into this."

"Which is the way we knew it would be." Gentry was putting down an irrational disappointment, having to tell himself that nothing could change things at this last moment. "But thanks for trying, Sergeant. Maybe there's no proof to get against him. My hunch could be wrong, 'way wrong."

"Or it could be dead right, sir. Caleb Ash could be brother to the devil and surprise no one. And he's hated you since the day you two met, when you turned down half his string of new remounts."

Gentry's wide shoulders lifted, fell. When he said nothing, McCune breathed furiously, "I know you're sick of goin' over it again and again, sir. But something's there, I tell you! Look at the money he made replacing those animals we lost last month. To hear him tell it, he handles remounts only as a sideline. Sideline, hell! He's cleared more on this last

9

sale than his livery and freightin' will make him over the next two years."

"That's still no proof of Caleb rigging the trouble I ran into," Gentry said quietly.

McCune sighed deeply, gustily. "Then there's this other, this about Lieutenant Fitzhugh. Why take that on your shoulders, too? Just because he was the major's son? Sir, fine as Major Fitzhugh is, there's just so much one man can do for another!"

"Look, Sergeant," the hardness that came to Gentry's glance then was prompted by the thought that the decision he'd made weeks ago, out there in that desert canyon and in sight of all the dead, was still the right one, "this is the way I want it, the way it's going to be. Nothing would be changed by smearing young Fitzhugh. That detail was wiped out except for the two of us. It was my gamble from the very beginning. Orders were disobeyed, and I was in command. If you —"

"But it was Lieutenant Fitzhugh, not you!" McCune cut in unthinkingly. His face reddened and he hastened to add, "If you'll excuse the mention of it again, sir."

"Sergeant, I'd hate ever having to call you a liar. But if you ever give me away by so much as a word — one word, mind you — that's what happens." Gentry's look abruptly softened. And now he spoke gently, saying,

"This will probably be our last chance for speaking privately, Tim. You've been fine all the way through. More than worth your stripes. You have my thanks for everything you've done."

"Which has turned out to be blessed little, Captain."

Gentry moved his head in a spare negative. "Hardly." His tone was utterly serious. "I could be off there in a grave alongside those eighteen others. You're the reason I'm not, and I'll never forget it. Never." He held out his hand then. "Now let's get on with this."

McCune reluctantly surrendered the saber and watched Gentry buckle it to belt. Then, as though the sight of that tall and erect shape pained him, he turned impatiently out into the corridor. Gentry followed in another moment, and both were silent as they walked on past the two other empty cells and through the deserted guardroom to its outer door.

Only there did McCune's sense of discipline desert him. He swung abruptly around and, without a word, took Gentry's right hand in both his own and wrung it fiercely. His blue eyes were moist, bright with a helpless anger as he turned then and stepped out the door, snapping hoarsely, " 'Ten'shun!"

Two troopers, privates, standing at either side of the gravelled path came to a ramrod stance. McCune waited until Gentry, momentarily blinded by the strong sunlight, had come out haltingly to stand between them. Then he said tonelessly, "Conduct the prisoner to the adjutant. Forward — March!"

There was a moment's confusion, McCune's having forgotten to give his men the order to shoulder their carbines. And Gentry, catching that, smiled thinly as they stepped on away from his sergeant toward the parade's edge. Then abruptly and for the first time everything out there came into sharp focus, sobering Gentry, awing him.

It was a bright summer day typical of the high country, warm but not hot, the air clear and bracing. Somewhere above in the timber a crow set up a raucous scolding to accent the stillness. It was the stillness more than anything else that first of all impressed Gentry.

Then, against the backdrop of the log buildings and high palisade, he saw K Troop drawn up beyond the flagpole in a precise line stretching toward the main gate. I Troop ranged the stableward length of the parade, its formation more ragged than K's. Major Fitzhugh's slight shape rigidly sat his big sorrel gelding at the center of an ordered rank of officers immediately behind the rock-ringed base of the flagpole. And as his guards now right-angled toward that group, Gentry caught the tight set of Fitzhugh's thin, sensitive face and was shocked by it pallor and the deep hurt it reflected.

He could no longer witness such a thing, and in trying to ignore it as he advanced he centered his attention on Sam Grell, adjutant, senior captain, and second in command. Grell stood alone and to this side of the flagpole, his expression one of flinty indignation, his ordinarily kind face brittle but lacking the wounded quality Fitzhugh's held. And Gentry, well knowing the man's usual gentleness and friendliness, once again moved his glance in search of something that didn't offend.

Then, through the gap between the two troops, he spied Caleb Ash.

Until this second he had been comparatively calm, anything but nervous, his conversation with McCune all but forgotten. But now instantly a towering rage mounted in him, and he could feel his stride falter, could sense that he was trembling.

Ash's massive frame stood leaning against the corner of Headquarters porch beyond a small group of somber-garbed women gathered on the walk. The man's indolent pose, so unmilitary against this precise setting, struck Gentry as being intentionally mocking and arrogant. He scarcely noticed that the liveryman and part-time civilian Army scout had dressed for the occasion, that Ash wore a gray derby, black coat, and white shirt in place of his customary buckskins. All that mattered to Gentry was that they had permitted the man to be here to witness his humiliation, probably to gloat over it. And he told himself, *Damn him, he's won!*

There was a sobering finality to that realization, one that quickly doused the blaze of his anger and left him hardly caring. A moment later he sensed that the interval over which he could so deliberately take in his surroundings was drawing to an end. And now, because everything about him seemed so alien, so unfriendly, he tried to forget that Ash stood across there and raised his glance along the slope of pine and aspen beyond the palisade toward the rocky heights of Sentinel.

Yet that vista, so cool and quiet and forever satisfying, was the thing that finally put beyond reach the stoicism he was groping for. And as the trooper on his left growled abruptly, "Detail-1 — halt!" to stop the trio at exactly the required two paces from Captain Grell, Gentry was feeling a bitterness that was deep and stark and unsettling.

This keen edge of emotion was knifing him as Sam Grell unfolded a sheet of paper and tonelessly began reading the Orders of the Day. So intently was Gentry trying to control

14

himself to the bearing of this moment that he almost missed the adjutant's words concerning him. Even then only snatches of the indictment penetrated his consciousness:

". . . conduct unbecoming of an officer and gentleman . . . This man knowingly and against orders sacrificed the lives of his fellow men in a criminal and foolhardy action . . . Thus, in carrying out the sentence of the courts-martial, Daniel Gentry shall thereafter be stripped of all honors, decorations, rank, and insignia. His name shall be stricken from the records of these honorable men. . . ."

Only when Sam Grell crumpled the sheet and threw it savagely aside did Gentry realize that the long-awaited moment was upon him. His former close friend and brother officer stepped up to him now and reached across to unbuckle the saber first of all, his tugs at the belt vicious, uncompromising. Grell put the saber under his left arm and then, beginning at the collar of Gentry's tunic, tore off the polished buttons. The epaulets were last of all, and the left one was stubborn and finally tore loose only after Grell had ripped the sleeve halfway from the shoulder seam.

Finished, Grell stood there, his glance lifting to meet Gentry's. Abruptly he spoke in a clear, angry voice that carried out over the parade. "I regret that regulations will not permit me to do violence upon you. I should like nothing better than to beat you with a cinch strap until you couldn't —"

A loud cough, Major Fitzhugh's, cut across his words. He set his jaw firmly and tossed aside the epaulets and the buttons. Then he took Gentry's saber from under arm, drew it from the scabbard, and, lifting a knee, broke the blade with a hard downthrust, the steel ringing a complaint against the warm stillness.

Gentry's glance was drawn irresistibly to Major Fitzhugh then as Sam Grell's voice intoned harshly, "Guard, conduct the prisoner to the gates!" And as both troopers laid a hold on his arms, giving no command now but simply pulling him away, Dan Gentry inwardly recoiled from the blue-eyed hate shining so brightly upon him out of his commanding officer's pallid countenance.

Almost at once the drums started a low, steady roll. And as Gentry and his two guards walked away from Grell and started along the ranks of K Troop, Gentry felt the full weight of his disgrace settling over him. Finally he brought his glance away from the faces he knew so well, having neither the strength of will nor the fortitude to stare out the open scorn he saw holding his men. In that instant he remembered Ash and, wondering how much the man had been able to see and hear of all this, resisted the urge to turn and look toward Headquarters.

The tone of the drums was vibrant and continuous, and all at once Gentry recognized in their hollow cadence the strains of the rogue's march, his imagination fitting the harsh and condemning notes of music to the insistent beat, the sound filling his head almost to bursting.

At length, mercifully, he was past the last in the long line of horses and men and alone with his guards. Yet now as he left the formation the roll of the drums seemed to take on a heavier beat, the sound dogging his heels, not letting the strain slacken. The nearest high shoulder of Sentinel picked up the throbbing note and threw it back in a pulsating crescendo of accusation. He hurried now, the chant of the drums driving out even the surface calmness that had stayed with him until this moment.

He finally caught himself on the very point of breaking into a run, caught a hold on his reason again. He slowed his stride, letting the two troopers come even with him. They walked on across to the gate that way, Gentry no longer finding the thunder of the drums so unbearable. Even the cackling laughs of the women standing by the huts along Laundry Row lost their sting of derision as they struck him. He was calm once more.

The sentry at the gate turned his back as they approached, kept it turned. Squarely in the gateway the two troopers shoved their prisoner roughly on ahead and stopped. Gentry found himself finally alone.

He went on along the town road until presently he could look out over the rim's edge and see the scars of the placers across the canyon below. The first buildings along the crooked street down there were just coming into sight when he unwittingly halted, all at once having heard the crunching of his boots against the gravel as an alien sound. Only then did he realize that the drums had gone silent.

Halfway surprised, he turned and looked back as a voice raised in command shuttled across the parade. He saw the formation breaking up, the big geldings swinging into a column of fours. The sentry and his two guards still stood in the gate. They were facing him, carbines in the bends of their arms, their stances purposely menacing.

Then as never before came the full realization of what had happened to him. Gentry felt unclean, really dishonored. And in this moment as his glance went beyond the gate he had the sight of Caleb Ash, standing there alone on the walk before Headquarters, to drive home the full weight of his disgrace.

Ash stood with long legs planted wide apart, hands on hips. The distance was far too great to be at all certain, but Gentry imagined he could read a broad grin on the man's ruddy face. And for a long moment it was all he could do to resist the urge to go back there, force his way through the gate and across the parade, to lay hands on Ash.

But in the end he somehow got a grip on himself and turned and walked on down the road with that same feeling of impotence he had learned to know so well over the past weeks.

Now all that remained was to leave this country for another where he could make a new start and begin forgetting.

A quarter-mile beyond Fort North the dust-smothered ruts of the road met a margin of tall lodgepoles and immediately swung out toward the rim's edge. From that point onward the wheel tracks dipped steeply along the winding cut made by Elk Creek in reaching the canyon bottom. And there, where the road was first closely flanked by the trees, a young woman stepped from behind a thicket of scrub oak and stood watching Gentry's approach.

There was an outright shock in her eyes at seeing the strangeness of his lagging stride, the way his hands were thrust deep in pockets, the vacant stare he fixed at the ground ahead of him. So stunned was she by his changed appearance that she let him get almost abreast of her before she remembered and called in a hushed, frightened way, "Captain!"

Dan Gentry stopped at once, her one word jarring him from his preoccupation and his glance shuttling across to her as a thin fog of dust, kicked up by his boots, overtook him. His lean face went slack with surprise at recognizing that slender and strongly feminine figure in its dress of unrelieved black. Instinctively he reached up to touch the brim of a hat he no longer wore, the gesture all the same gracious, courteous as he drawled, "You, Mrs. Fitzhugh!"

For a moment she stared at him wide-eyed and hurt at seeing how disheveled he looked with the torn sleeve and his blouse hanging open. Then a forced smile rid her pale oval face of its bewilderment and turned it quite beautiful. She held out a hand, beckoning him. "Back here," she said softly, "where no one will see us."

"Of course." He couldn't help putting an even dryer edge to his tone as he added, "You shouldn't be seen with a pariah like me."

"Dan, it's not that!" she breathed as he started toward her. "It's — you see, I told the major I couldn't bear to be there, told him I was going down to the dressmaker's when really I'd planned all along on meeting you. Sergeant McCune thought you'd be needing clothes. And a gun." Her head with its small black hat perched on her high-piled ebony hair tilted toward the trees. "I have them here. McCune thought it best not to tell you."

Gentry's soberness eased somewhat as he came up to her. "I could use a new outfit."

She reached out impulsively then and took his hand, leading him on around the thicket until they were within sight of a horse and buggy standing back among the trees. And she asked uncertainly, "Was it — awful back there?"

"Nothing I won't get over."

His strictly neutral tone made her look around at him, an oddly beseeching quality in her glance. Then quite unexpectedly she stopped and turned to grip his arms tightly in her slender hands. "You mustn't let it change you, Dan! Never be any other than you've always been!"

Some barrier she had raised against her emotions gave way then. She drew closer to him and, bowing her head to his chest, began sobbing brokenly, softly. He was bewildered and embarrassed, and as her body trembled against him he put a hand to the back of her head, saying gruffly, "It's done with, Mrs. Fitzhugh. Let's forget it."

"Forget it?" Her head rocked back, pale cheeks glistening with tears. "How can it be forgotten? There's been some horrible mistake! I — it hurts me terribly to see this happening to you."

"The Army doesn't make mistakes, Mrs. Fitzhugh."

"Mrs. Fitzhugh?" she echoed wonderingly. "Are we still such strangers that you can't yet call me by my given name?"

He was uneasily trying to give her an answer when she spoke again, letting him know she had expected none. "You're wrong in what you say. The Army does make mistakes, many of them. This is one. It will never be the same for you. Never!"

"Why not?" He lifted his broad, heavy shoulders in a careless shrug, even grinning faintly in a way that held a quality of real amusement. "By tonight I'll be gone, Mary. By next week I'll have found something else. Twenty-seven is young enough to make a new start. And —"

"And you can't just shed this life as you would a coat." Anger and rebellion were giving her cheeks more color now.

"If a coat wears out you can shed it." He was having no more of this pointless argument and glanced toward the buggy. "That outfit McCune sent. Is it in the rig?"

"Yes. In back."

Her tone held a lifeless quality that let him know she had expected a far different reaction from him. Yet he stubbornly left her and walked over to the buggy. He pulled a bundle of clothes, a heavy shell belt and gun, and a wide, curl-brimmed hat from the box behind the seat. Looking back at her then with a nod of thanks he went on around the rig.

He had shrugged off the blue blouse and was pulling the belt from his yellow-striped trousers when she called, "Dan, there are some things you should know before you leave."

"What things?"

"First, that Phil was a coward."

Her unexpected words jolted him so hard that his hands hung motionless, holding the clean but worn waist-overalls he had taken from the bundle. He asked himself, *Can she know?* and over his wonderment managed to say, "Any son of Robert Fitzhugh a coward? You're wrong, dead wrong. You've heard how they found him, the —"

"I know all that," her voice interrupted. "The Apaches lying all about him, the arrow in his back. But I tell you he was a coward!"

She hesitated, giving him the chance to speak. When he didn't she went on. "Something happened to him when he got his orders, long before we left Leavenworth. He raged when he heard they were sending him out here. Even the unofficial reason of his father's health made no impression whatsoever on him. He was deathly afraid at the prospect of campaigning against the Apaches. And he was white with fear that night he left with you, his first and only action. He'd been drinking for days, Dan, drinking a lot. Perhaps you knew it, perhaps not. And he was coarse, beastly when he drank. I — So what came out at your courts-martial about how they found him made no sense!"

"But, damn it, it was there for everyone to see!"

Gentry buckled on his gun belt, then buttoned the gray flannel shirt that looked and felt as strange as the tight-fitting denims. And now he snatched up the brown wool coat and wide hat McCune had sent him and, holding his uniform wadded in the other hand, came from behind the buggy.

Mary Fitzhugh's look was startled as she took in the change in him. It was a long moment before she managed to say, "Yes, it was there for everyone to see. But I shall never believe that Phil died any other way than as a complete coward."

"Isn't there a saying, 'Speak no ill of the dead,' Mary?" he drawled quietly, leaning over to tie the sagging holster unnaturally low along his thigh.

"I've spoken it, Dan," she stated deliberately. "I have no regrets."

A real anger all at once brightened the darkness of his eyes. "If the major should ever hear of this, should even suspect —"

She waited a moment after his words had trailed off helplessly. Then: "The major never will hear of it. Not from me."

"It would kill him. Kill him just as surely as though George Spires were to give him strychnine instead of medicine! He must never have the slightest inkling of what you thought of Phil. If you should ever —"

"But I've told you I never will!" she spoke heatedly. Yet there was a tenderness in her tone as she added, "You love him, don't you, Dan?"

Gentry eyed her then in such an outraged way that she could scarcely believe her eyes. It was as though she had touched upon something he considered inviolate, something so purely personal to him that it seemed she had betrayed a trust in even mentioning it.

"I do," he said deliberately. "If I had a father, one I could even remember, I would want him to be like Robert Fitzhugh."

"I'm sorry," she murmured. "I was only trying to tell you that I understand, that you can trust me."

"Mary, I served under him during the War. I was fifteen then and I worshiped him. Maybe you know that he later made it possible for me to go to the Academy. But neither of those things count. Nor does it count that he's taught me everything I know about real soldiering." His tone had lost its cutting edge, and now he added very soberly, "It's that he — that they don't come any finer. I would do anything to save him a moment's pain."

She gave him an odd, measuring glance. "Do you think what's happened to you has saved him pain?"

She caught the instant hardening of his expression and quickly put in, "That was an unkind thing to say. Please forgive me." Her eyes pleaded with him and shortly, when she saw his anger fading, she asked, "Would you like to hear the rest, Dan? I had only commenced."

"Is there more?" he asked guardedly.

"Yes. I must tell you about myself. Before you ask why, I'll say that it's simply because I very much want you to know. You above all others."

The implication to those words made him uncomfortable, and she saw that and went on. "For over a year now, long before we came here, I've simply existed. Not lived, existed! Had I had a family, anyone to turn to, I would have left Phil. He and I had become complete strangers to each other."

"Do husbands and wives ever agree on everything?"

"On the basic things, yes. We didn't have even those in common. It would be despicable of me to add anything to that. But we weren't even friends."

Gentry shook his head in a perplexed way. "No one would have guessed it."

"No. We had made a pact to spare the major's feelings. There was at least enough decency in Phil for that. Or perhaps it was fear. I've never known."

"The Old Man doesn't have it in him to make anyone afraid of him, Mary."

"Then I'm wrong. But at any rate I've kept a bargain, played out a part. You're the only one who knows the truth or even suspects how I loathe this dress." She lifted her arms outward and glanced down at her slender, gently rounded body in its sheath of severe black. "This mourning! What a mockery it is!"

Her gesture, so plainly inviting his attention, brought home to him in that moment her undeniably strong physical attractions; and for the first time he was realizing fully that she was an extremely desirable woman no longer claimed by another man. Yet he was again uneasy over the direction her words were taking and without pausing to weigh the oddness of his feeling he said, "I wish there were something I could say to convince you how wrong you are about Phil."

"There is nothing you could say that would convince me of that." She let her hands fall to her sides again. "But underneath, beneath this accursed black, I'm free, Dan! I can begin to live again."

Over a moment's strained silence he said awkwardly, "Maybe I know how you feel. I'm trying to look at things that —"

His words broke off as he caught the rhythmic hoof-falls of a horse sounding from close by along the road. And, thankful for the interruption, he looked on out through the trees and then stepped past Mary Fitzhugh and over behind the oak thicket.

From there he watched a big, rangy bay gelding walk slowly into sight from beyond the far edge of the dense oak brush. Even before the tangle of brush let him make out the massive shape in the saddle he recognized the animal and knew the rider to be Caleb Ash. And at once he was feeling a surge of the cold fury that had lately come whenever he set eyes on the man or even thought of him.

His impulse then was to step from behind the thicket and into the road, to bring on a showdown he had often prayed he might some day have with Ash. Yet he halfway hesitated, thinking of Mary Fitzhugh being here. And abruptly that hesitation jelled before a baffled helplessness as he told himself, *You haven't a shred of proof!*

The next moment, his impulse bridled, he was feeling a strong puzzlement at the expression he read on Ash's craggy face. Instead of the satisfied smile or the look of gloating he had expected, he saw the man scowling glumly, staring worriedly down at the road ahead. And as Gentry wondered at this Ash rode on past.

The rage in Gentry was dying now and with his last glimpse of the scout, before the bay walked out of sight around the road's lower bend, he admitted grudgingly that the man made an imposing and impressive bulk regardless of the outlandish clothes.

Ash was barely out of sight when Gentry caught a rustle of sound behind him and turned to find Mary Fitzhugh standing almost within arm-reach. And as his glance met hers she asked, "He was there?"

When he only nodded, she put another question. "He wasn't your friend, was he?"

"No."

She seemed uninterested in his reply, in fact gave no sign that she had heard it as she stared beyond him soberly, almost sadly. He sensed

29

that she was making a last attempt at calling back that earlier mood even before she murmured, "If I could only be going away with you, Dan. I would give anything for that."

He put a serious look upon her. "And leave the major, sick as he is?"

She colored at the accusation in his tone and, her pride visibly stiffening, she coolly said, "You take me too literally. Of course I'm staying with him. But I can still envy you, can't I?"

He was thankful for the turn their words were taking and said wryly, "No one else does, Mary."

She ignored his meaning and abruptly, holding out her hand, she said, "I suppose this is our good-by."

He took her hand, answering its firm pressure. And she told him, "One more thing, Dan. You must write me. I want to know where you are, how you are."

He nodded. "Yes. I had intended writing. I'd like to hear how it goes with the major."

Only when he saw her wince did he realize how unfairly he had spoken. And he hastened to add, "I'll also be wanting to know about you, Mary."

The smile she gave him was empty of all amusement. "I had hoped you would."

Just then he was wanting more than any-

That first summer Mike Clears stumbled into the wisest move he had ever made in a business way. He hired an Indian-raised white, an older man, off the reservation. After Ben Qualls had been with him several weeks, the Apaches began trading despite the presence of the soldiers. Later it was Qualls who talked him into building permanently down here rather than going above to locate near the post gates, Qualls insisting that the hostiles would put more trust in a trader if he showed his independence of the Army. They had.

Accident, nothing but, changed Mike Clears from trader to saloonman. This had happened only last summer. A close-mouthed crewman of Ash's who had spent his spare time gouging the slopes behind the layout one day turned up missing, leaving Ash short a driver on one of his new freight-hitches. Later, when the stampede began, Ash learned what had happened to his man. He had ridden across to Taos, gone on a three-day bout with the bottle, and talked a tall story. As a consequence of his producing a pokeful of yellow dust to convince his doubters, a considerable rabble and a sprinkling of real prospectors poured in shortly afterward.

The newcomers bought anything and everything Mike Clears had to sell, particularly

thing else to wipe out this awkwardness between them. Yet, unable to think of anything he might say that would accomplish that, he looked down at the uniform he still held in his hand. He lazily tossed it into the oak brush, turning from her as he drawled, "Thank McCune for the outfit. And I wish you luck, you and the major." He hesitated, looked around. "Good-by, Mary."

He was walking away from her when she said softly, "Good-by — Dan."

He sensed the catch in her voice and didn't look around. Only when he had reached the road's lower bend and knew he must be out of her sight did he draw in a deep breath and let it out in a long, slow sigh of relief.

Chapter Two

The placers along Elk Creek had in little more than a year changed the look of the canyon immediately below Fort North. Where once there had been nothing but Mike Clears's log trading-post and, above it, the sprawling sheds and corrals of Caleb Ash's horse ranch, there now stretched between the two a disorderly array of tents, pole and tar-paper shacks, and a few substantial cabins. Newcomers were calling the settlement Elk Bend.

The placers, most of them below town, scarred the canyon's far side beyond the willow-edged creek well up each finger-draw snaking back into the higher hills. Isolated by upward of a hundred miles of hostile land between here and the nearest civilized country around Sante Fe, the diggin's had attracted only the hardiest prospectors, men who worked with rifles leaning against their sluiceways and rocker boxes, men who could shoot. There would be a real boom here one day, but only after the more incorrigible Apaches gave up their habit of periodically breaking off the reservation.

Mike Clears had come here in his twenty-fourth year, five years ago, bringing two wagonloads of trade goods under the protection of an Army survey party and its escort trying to locate a new post along the newly established reservation's eastern boundary. Both Clears and the surveyors found the canyon to their liking, the soldiers because the timbered bench above edged by its rim dropping a sheer three hundred feet into the canyon exactly suited their purpose, Clears because the prospect of trade with both hostiles and whites was too good a chance to pass up.

Mike Clears's first winter in the canyon put

considerable maturity on him. By a vast amount of effort he and his two drivers dismantled the wagons and moved them, his goods, and teams into a deep cave in the rim face below the bench. They had logged up the cave mouth by the time the Army pulled out. Throughout the long cold months they never left the cave singly. And for several weeks the following spring when a band of Jicarillas camped below along the canyon they didn't stir from their crude fort and lived o[n] a diet of horsemeat.

In late spring when the cavalry and a civili[an] work-party returned, Clears and his men mov[ed] into the canyon with them, and Clears star[ted] the erection of a sizable cabin. It was less [than] a month later that Caleb Ash arrived [with] a herd of horses, unannounced and unbi[dden.] The amiable giant, seeming in some ways [more] Indian than white, had gambled shrew[dly on] the Army's need for draft animals. The [gamble] immediately paid off when Ash was gi[ven a] logging contract on the new construct[ion.]

By the following year, when the pe[rmanent] garrison arrived, Ash had built a larg[e barn] and had on hand a string of big, s[olid-] color geldings ideal for remounts. [Of all] the animals the cavalry brought w[ith them] there hadn't been a gelding in the [cavalry] since then that hadn't come from A[sh—ev]ery

32

33

his whisky. So when he freighted in more supplies he concentrated on wet goods rather than dry. Now he was calling his establishment the *Lucky Find* and no longer stocked anything but whisky, tobacco, and cards.

Again it was by pure accident that Clears found himself now running what the local folk were calling a hotel. When the boom first started, men began offering a dollar a night for the comfort of getting in out of the weather and sleeping in Clears's sod-roofed barn across the road from his main building. Presently, seeing the possibilities, Clears moved his livestock and stored goods up to the cave he had called home that first winter. Then he pulled off the barn's rotten earth roof, covered it over with canvas stretched across a new ridge log, tore out the stalls, and built fourteen double bunks of aspen poles and rope. Over the barn's door this spring he had painted a big sign, *Sleep Here*. Inside, along a crude counter in the entryway, hung another sign that bore a longer legend:

Sleep Eight Hours for a Dollar!
Good Beds.
Shifts change Noon, Eight Night, Four
Morning
Pay As You Turn In
QUIET ! !

Today, Clears had spent most of the morning in his bunk barn supervising the building of another dozen two-decker beds. Consequently he hadn't heard the roll of the drums from above that had puzzled many people along the street. Now, as the noon hour approached, his appetite brought him onto the street wondering idly if Ben Qualls had anything at the *Lucky Find*'s eat-counter besides the everlasting same offering of roast wild turkey and venison haunch. He was stepping from the crowded plank walk, about to cross over to his saloon, when he saw Caleb Ash riding toward him close ahead.

The man's outlandish appearance told him at once where Ash had been; and with a faint exasperation he remembered as he had several other times this morning that this was no ordinary day up at the fort. He could have gone up there, perhaps should have put in an appearance. But he'd wanted to have nothing more to do with the affair. He didn't even want to know what had happened.

He was hoping Ash wouldn't see him. Ordinarily he and the liveryman were civil enough to each other and little more, for he had respect but little liking for the man. Yet now as he started turning away with the thought of making himself inconspicuous among the passers-by, Ash spotted him and at once reined his way.

So Clears made the best of it, smiling broadly and calling, "Where's your Bible, Caleb? You could be brother to that sky pilot we had up here last summer. Where'd you pick up the fancy rig?"

Ash stopped the bay close alongside, his tanned face taking a deeper flush. But for once he was enjoying a joke on himself and, grinning ruefully, he growled, "Reckon I do look the fool." Then, abruptly sobering, he asked, "Why wasn't you up there, Mike?"

Clears sighed and shook his head. "I'm trying to forget the whole thing."

"They did it up brown. He was like a whipped cur, tail tucked when they turned him loose."

A faint anger stirred in Clears. "Why couldn't they just let him go without all the damn formality?"

"Just let him go?" Ash snorted. "Why, if I'd had the doin' of it, they'd have strung him up!" He caught the look in Clears's eyes then. Warned by it, he shrugged, drawling in a milder tone, "Anyway, it's done with and done proper." He thought of something else, asking querulously, "Say, how long's it going to take Tipton to get his wagons here? Now I wish I'd hauled that hardware all that way myself. Here I've got the roof on the new store and nothin' to put in it."

"Tipton'll be along in his own good time," Clears said. "It's a hard haul, this last stretch. He must be short-handed. Otherwise that man he sent up with that word for us yesterday wouldn't't've turned around and gone on back."

Ash's scowl didn't ease as he grunted, "I just been down the road a piece, couple miles or so, thinkin' I might meet up with the wagons. But nothin's in sight. Every extra day he takes sure costs me money." He lifted rein then, and as the bay went on he called back, "Tell Qualls to save me a plate of food."

Clears nodded and stood there watching the big man ride on, this fresh reminder of Dan Gentry bringing back that familiar sense of baffling inadequacy in even beginning to understand the findings of the courts-martial. Weeks ago, on first hearing of Gentry's arrest, he had been shocked and hurt. He had long known Dan Gentry as a kind, warmhearted, and generous man, honest to the core. He simply knew, without having to understand quite why, that his friend couldn't be guilty of the things he stood accused of. Yet the court found that Gentry, attacked by Apaches, had, in direct disobedience to orders, taken his men into a canyon where they were all killed except Gentry himself and Sergeant McCune. It just didn't make sense to Clears.

He went on into the *Lucky Find* now and made his way through the crowd to the back end of the bar. Ben Qualls was there, slicing breast meat from a steaming turkey carcass. He didn't look up when Clears stepped to the counter. Yet, with his instinct for knowing exactly what was going on around him without seeming to observe it, he said as Clears put his elbows on the polished wood, "Better toss him out, Mike," nodding toward the front of the crowded room.

Clears looked up there, couldn't understand. "Who?" he asked.

"Gentry."

Clears's glance sharpened. Abruptly he saw Gentry, not the tall uniformed shape but an unfamiliar one crowned by a gray Stetson and shrouded in a rumpled brown coat.

"When did he get here, Ben?"

"Half hour ago. Bought a quart jug right off."

"A quart?" Clears's eyes opened wider. "Hell, man, he's no drinker!"

"He is today, Mike."

The saloonman stood deliberating a moment, a strong embarrassment crowding him. Then, knowing what he must do, he made his way through the crowd between bar and poker layouts and came in behind Gentry to tap him on the shoulder.

When Gentry turned, Clears tilted his head toward the rear of the room, saying only, "Come along, Dan," before he started back there. And Gentry, faintly scowling at first, then as faintly smiling, followed.

Beyond the end of the bar was the door to Clears's office. He opened it wide and stepped aside for Gentry to enter first. Following the taller man on into the room, he closed the door and leaned back against it.

"Ben says you bought a jug," he said mildly. "How come?"

Gentry eyed him coolly a moment. Then, with a shrug, he turned across the room toward a door that let out onto the saloon's alley platform. "You don't have to say it, Mike," he drawled dryly. "I'll leave. Maybe Belle'll let me kill time at her place."

"Hold on!" Clears's words stopped Gentry, made him look around. Then the saloonman said quietly, "My friend, you can't do this. Belle's place or mine, it makes no difference. Someone's going to choose you before the day's out."

Gentry only smiled, and shortly Clears went on. "You probably wouldn't mind a scrap. You could tear this place apart and I wouldn't mind it either if you had any fun doing it. But it's yourself you'd be breaking

40

up, Dan. Don't do it."

"There's seven hours to kill before the stage pulls out."

"Then go up to the cave and stay out of sight. If it's whisky you want, help yourself. There's plenty up there. I'll even go up the street and buy your stage ticket so you won't run into trouble —"

The rattle of the latch behind him cut across Clears's words, and all at once the door swung open, catching him hard between the shoulders. He wheeled quickly around, cursing softly, growling, "Knock before you come in that —" going silent when he saw who stood there.

It was Tim McCune's blocky shape that moved in through the door. He saw Gentry, stiffened in startlement, then saluted. Gentry soberly touched his hat. Then McCune, his face redder than usual and his breathing fast and plainly audible, moved aside so that a second man, a stranger, could step into the doorway.

McCune's look had been excited; yet it seemed Gentry's presence changed that excitement to something else. For when he spoke it was almost casually to say, "Mike, we've got the 'Paches with us again." He looked around at his companion then, adding, "You tell it, Shotwell."

41

The other man leaned against the doorframe now as though about to collapse. His thin, beard-stubbled face wore a gaunt look of utter exhaustion. His eyes were red-rimmed, his shirt was torn and darkly stained, and the hand he lifted to his face was trembling.

"They caught our wagons ten miles below, mister," he said in a voice dry as dust, "Finished off all our people and —"

"Not Tipton's wagons!" Clears cut in hoarsely.

"Who else's?" Shotwell replied. "They got us all, all but me. Worst thing I ever set eyes to. We heard as how these hostiles up here never took scalps. But they sure took 'em today. God, you could hear 'em tear loose! The worst was the women. Then's when I got sick and —"

"Women?" Clears echoed, his face wearing a gray look. "What women?"

"The boss's missus and his girl. And one other young one."

Clears turned away to step across and lean heavily against his desk, saying incredulously, "Harry Tipton dead? And not four months ago he was here, right here in this room —" His words trailed off and, straightening with an obvious effort to get a hold on himself, he looked at McCune. "What is it you want of me, Tim?"

42

"There's some freight of Ash's and yours in the wagons, Mike," McCune answered quietly. "A billiard table, some bales of tobacco for you. We've located Ash. Lieutenant Peebles is taking a detail down there right away. He thought you two'd better be along."

"The freight be damned!" Clears burst out. Then, his look an apology, he added in a quieter tone, "No, Tim, I don't want to see it. Go on without me."

McCune, after a brief and hesitant glance at Gentry, stepped back through the door, asking Shotwell, "You still not coming?"

"And see that all over again? Hunh-uh!" Shotwell was eyeing Clears now and said awkwardly, "Mister, my poke's down there in one of the wagons. Could you stake me to the loan of a dollar or two so's I can buy a bed across the way to sleep in? I spent half the mornin' hid in the brush. Then hoofin' it all this way got me so played out I —"

"Here," Clears said. He had reached to a pocket as the man was speaking and now came across to hand him a double eagle.

Shotwell's glance momentarily lost its lifeless quality as he smiled delightedly. "Thanks," he said. "Thanks muchly, friend." And he turned and followed McCune out.

The door had barely swung shut when Gentry started for the alley once again. His hand was reaching for the knob when Clears said quietly, "Wait!"

Gentry looked around to find the saloonman eyeing him soberly, speculatively. It was a long moment before Clears said, "There goes your stage ride. Now what'll you do?"

Gentry said evenly, "I'll make out."

"What will you do?" Clears insisted. "You can't buy a horse in this town from anyone but Ash. And he'd see you crawl out of here before he sold you one."

"Then I'll crawl."

Clears gave a slow shake of the head. "You'd never make it on foot."

"Then I'll hang around till the scare's over."

Again the saloonman shook his head. "That's the one thing you can't do." His look held Gentry's briefly, beseechingly almost, before he added, "Go on up to the cave and take that old *grulla*. She's wind-broke, and if you run onto trouble she won't be much help. But if you keep out of sight and ease through that country at night she'll carry you as far as Sante Fe. A McClellan's hanging right ahead of her stall. Take it, too."

An oddly puzzled look crossed Gentry's face. "How come you're not hangin' in with the rest, Mike?"

"I've never turned on a friend," Clears stated. "I'm even wishing you luck."

44

Gentry laughed softly, mockingly. "You're alone in your sentiments." As an afterthought he reached to the inside pocket of his coat and drew out a wallet. "How much do I owe you?"

Clears shook his head, stepping across to the alley door and opening it. "Nothing," he said. "The mare isn't worth her keep, and that hull's the hardest I ever sat. Be glad to get rid of them both."

Gentry came on past him and out onto the platform. He paused there to drawl, "Much obliged, Mike."

"Dan, is there —" Clears was wordless a moment, obviously ill at ease. Then: "Is there anything you could tell me about — Hell, it's more than a man can take in!"

Gentry deliberated his answer, warding off his first impulse by telling himelf, *Keep it to yourself, it's nearly over.* He said finally, "No, there's nothing to tell, Mike. So long." And he went out and down the platform steps and across the alley.

He felt as alone as he ever had when shortly he heard the saloon door close behind him. Just now he wanted nothing so much as Mike Clears's respect, and he doubted he had even that. Clears had been sympathetic, generous. That was all. He was a man whose feelings were hard to read, and it galled Gentry to have to leave without the one man above all he valued as a friend knowing the truth about him. These were his thoughts as he walked down to the plank footbridge over the creek and then up the narrow shelf road leading to the cave in the rim's face.

The still coolness of the cave was soothing after the strong sunlight outside; and as Gentry took his time saddling the *grulla* mare, most of the rancor and hurt in him quieted. Presently he could begin looking ahead to the next few days and consider rationally what the Apache outbreak might mean to him. Two years of campaigning against this particular tribe had given him more than a slight knowledge of them; and now, thinking of the leaders, he knew without the slightest doubt that *Gonah-Dokoh,* "Sour Eye," must have led the renegades in their latest outrage.

Sour Eye was the biggest troublemaker of recent years. There was no shred of mercy in him for the white man. He refused any contact with a white, would even send one of his sons or one of his wives to the agency to claim his beef issue. He stayed on the reservation only at such times as he was gathering the malcontents about him and equipping them for his next raid. Only the ineptness and caviling of officials in Washington had prevented his capture and imprisonment.

Considering the long ride he was about to take, Gentry judged he would have at the most only half a day's grace, till sundown today, before he would be in dangerous country. Sour Eye's band might haunt the trails and the one road for the next day or so, counting on easy plunder. So tonight Gentry would travel as far as he could and spend the dawn hour finding a place to hide out tomorrow's daylight. Because of the Apaches the distance to Sante Fe had become immeasurably greater, and he would need luck to arrive there.

The *grulla* saddled, Gentry led her out toward the cave mouth, past a high mound of wild hay reaching toward the rocky dome twenty feet overhead, past Clears's new buggy and a weathered buckboard. Well back from the cave mouth was a row of whisky barrels and in front of them some glass-fronted counters Clears had discarded when he changed over his store.

Gentry tied the mare below in the alley and entered the rear of a store. Some twenty minutes later he was back lugging a sack filled with grub, a Spencer carbine under one arm, a blanket and ground-sheet under the other. He made a tight roll of his purchases and, after tying the roll on behind the saddle's cantle, mounted and rode on down the alley.

At the foot of the bench road he turned and

looked back. His glance scarcely touched the clutter of buildings in the canyon bed, instead lifting for a final and reluctant glimpse of Fort North. All he could see beyond the edge of the high rim was one corner of the log palisade and, farther in, a line of wash flapping in the gentle breeze behind the hutments along Laundry Row.

His eye had already swung away from that drab scene when abruptly something he had noticed took it back again. And now, beyond the line of wash, he was seeing the tip of the flagpole at the center of the parade, the colors drooping from it.

The flag was so positioned that it seemed to be hanging from the wash line with the shirts and socks and underwear fluttering there. The irony of that sight, the suggestion of that splendid and inspiring symbol hanging where it appeared to be, struck Gentry as a farewell sight eloquently in keeping with his going. And as he turned on down the road he was vastly thankful to be leaving all this behind him.

Once below the placers he had the road to himself. Word of the reservation break had evidently spread quickly, for there was neither man nor animal in sight. This tonic of being free and alone was something he had long looked forward to; and strangely, now that he was on the way out, he found most of his resentment gone. He wasn't letting himself think back upon a single thing. He was trying to think ahead.

Only once over the next hour was his solitary, slow ride intruded upon. He had gone perhaps six leisurely miles when he met Peebles's detail escorting a light spring wagon up the road. He had plenty of warning, and by the time the troopers rode into sight he was on the far side of the creek, well hidden in the timber.

He watched the column trot smartly past, big Caleb Ash in his buckskins and Peebles in his blue uniform leading the others. He was close enough to identify each man and, shortly, to make out the two even rows of blanket-wrapped shapes roped to the wagon's sideless bed as it drew on past.

Sobered by that sight, he cut back to the road wondering what his own luck was to be over the next three or four days in crossing that wild and unfriendly waste of country beyond the foothills.

Going on down the canyon in the thinning dust-haze of the detail's passage, he was thinking of the ceremony that would doubtless be taking place tomorrow morning at the post cemetery. Major Fitzhugh would read the service over the graves. Or, if he wasn't feeling up to it, Doc Spires would take his place. They both had a flair for words. And in imagining where the graves would be Gentry could too plainly see other fresh earth mounds, eighteen of them; and in that moment a bleak, chill feeling settled through him.

He had ridden another two miles when, rounding a shoulder of the canyon wall, he came upon the first wagon. It lay there on its side so closely and abruptly ahead of him that sight of it stiffened him in the saddle.

It was a Conestoga. In overturning it had disgorged a disorderly litter of bales and barrels and boxes that lay strewn across the grassy creek bank. The torn edges of its split-open tarp flapped gently in the breeze. Gentry noticed an arrow sticking in the seat's back rest. He saw cut harness lying on the grass as he rode on.

Shortly he came upon the others, three more Conestogas, the last overturned as had been the first, its hickory top-bows broken so that the canvas shrouded half the spilled contents. The wagons were strung out, all headed in the same up-canyon direction, and it was at once obvious to Gentry how complete the Apache surprise had been. This stretch of the ravine was narrow, and the road closely flanked to both sides by timber. There hadn't even been time for the luckless teamsters to begin forming a defensive circle of their big, lumbering vehicles.

That last wagon, when he came even with it, held Gentry's attention the longest. There had been something impersonal about the others, particularly the first with its spilled merchandise. But this last one was different. He could see an oak bureau lying on its side, there was a cherry-wood desk of unusually fine lines standing upright and, beyond it, two white-painted iron bedsteads and a brass-bound chest with its burst-open lid all but hidden by the edge of the canvas. Harry Tipton had evidently planned to make Elk Bend his home.

Gentry wouldn't have lingered if he hadn't noticed a big metal canteen wrapped in gunny sacking that hung from the sky-tilted side of that last Conestoga. Here was something he could use. And he reined the mare over there with the thought that the canteen could save him many detours for water over the next few days in crossing the dry country beyond the hills.

As he was swinging lazily aground, the *grulla* all at once shied violently. Gentry was nearly thrown and did his best to steady her, drawling, "Easy, girl! Whoa!" But the animal, so utterly placid until this moment, only tossed her head and tried to pull away. Gentry shortened his hold on the reins and laid a hand on her shoulder, hoping to quiet her. But she reared and struck out at him with her hoofs.

In the end he led the mare across the wheel ruts and tied her to a pine sapling. And as he sauntered back over to the wagon to get the canteen he was more than ever curious over what had frightened the animal. He decided finally that it must have been sunlight reflected from the broken pieces of a mirror lying near the chest. And, eyeing the glass, he stepped closer, trying to place himself where the mare had been.

It was in this moment that he caught a whisper of sound rising over the creek's steady murmur. It lacked all definition. He stood very still, breathing shallowly, listening. Suddenly it came again from a point close ahead of him. It was a faint, smothered outcry.

He stepped quickly into the litter and reached out to take a hold on the edge of the canvas and throw it back. He looked down at the chest's inner edge, at its spilled top tray. What he saw froze his big frame in a paralysis of amazement.

At first it appeared to be nothing but a rumpled length of yard goods, of red-and-blue-printed calico showing from beneath the trunk. But then he saw the wavy mass of tawny golden hair beyond the trunk's back edge.

He moved fast now, lifting the trunk by

its handles and heaving it aside. He went to his knees, staring down in bewilderment at a huddled form.

What held his glance longest was a streak of bright crimson snaking down from that mass of golden hair across the girl's face that was serene and beautiful.

It was when Dan Gentry lifted her and carried her into the shade at the head of the wagon that Faith Tipton's awareness surged from out of the drowned depths of unconsciousness and almost reached the surface of understanding. From some remote recess of her mind cried a voice of fear and pain she knew she should be listening to and dully, over a space of indeterminate time, she tried to heed it.

But all through her was a languor she couldn't rouse from. It numbed her will and wouldn't let her respond at those infrequent times when she heard a voice, a strange one, a man's, speaking to her. Not only did it seem unimportant to know who he might be but she wasn't even interested in knowing what he was saying. She did somehow grasp the fact that his voice sounded friendly. That in itself seemed sufficient, all she could wish for.

The refreshing shock of her face being bathed with cold water brought her a brief and lucid moment in which she plainly caught the sound of Gentry's breathing close above her face. But an instant later he began wiping away the blood caked on the ugly gash high along her forehead, and the pain of it made her cry out. And once more her senses were numbed, and she slipped back into unconsciousness.

Her next full awareness came against a sickening swaying of her body, and it took a definite strength of will to push aside the heavy, cottony throbbing of her head and alert her senses. Then she could distinguish certain sounds, a horse's slow hoofbeat, the creak of saddle leather. Her body felt cramped, and she was aware of her shoulders being tightly held. When she finally understood that she was being carried on the back of a horse, that someone was holding her, outright terror made her open her eyes.

She was staring up into a man's lean face. It was tanned but not dark enough to belong to an Apache. He wasn't looking at her. And gradually her fright drained away as she studied his clean-lined features and the friendliness of his eyes, a deep brown. Over the next several seconds as her thoughts hung suspended there was little emotion in her beyond a thankfulness at being able to see objects and relate herself to them so as to quiet the queeziness of her stomach.

Then suddenly it all came back to her, and

across her mind's eye there flashed a host of frightening images. She saw again the fleeting shadows materializing out of the dawn-lighted timber beside the road, she heard the abrupt thunder of the guns, the high-pitched cries of the Apaches. Worst of all was the vision of her father suddenly lurching erect from the seat ahead of where she lay, clawing at his chest, and afterward falling brokenly down between the lunging wheel horses. Then the wagon was tilting crazily over onto its side, and she was crying out in panic and horror.

Gentry's face tilted quickly down. "You're all right," he said gently, tightening rein on the *grulla*. And as the motion of the horse stopped, he smiled down at her. "This is better. You had me worried."

There was in Faith Tipton a reserve of quiet strength, and she drew upon it now, getting herself in hand. For some obscure reason she decided it was important not to show any hysteria or feminine weakness to this man. She would have liked to sit straighter and ease the cramp in her back. But it also seemed important not to move and lose the reassuring strength of his arm about her shoulders.

She kept her voice firm and even as she asked, "Where are you taking me?"

"To a doctor, an Army sawbones. Just a couple more miles and we'll be there — if this mare holds out."

She remembered now and asked, "Fort North?"

He nodded.

She was remembering other things, yet dreading his answers if she should mention them. He interrupted her thoughts then, asking, "D'you want anything? A drink, maybe?"

"Nothing."

"Is your head all that hurts?"

She wasn't listening. There was something she had to know, and she was trying to summon the courage to ask him about it. And in another moment she had found the courage and looked up at him to breathe haltingly, "Mother and — and Dad. And the others. Where are they?"

His glance lifted quickly away. "Let's wait to talk about that, miss. Right now the best thing's to —"

She had read enough into his look to understand completely. Her choked, forlorn cry was barely audible. And as he told her, "We'll go along now. Just don't move or you'll slide off," she was trembling as though gripped by a sudden chill.

It was a long time before the tears came, long after the steady swaying motion of the *grulla* had resumed. She turned her head then and put her face against the rough material of Gentry's coat, crying silently, spending her strength in fighting against making any sound. And presently the shock and the rigid way she was holding herself exhausted her so completely that she mercifully dropped off into a half-sleep that dulled her terror.

Only once before Gentry lifted her down from the mare's back at dusk before Doc Spires's quarters on the post was she really aware of anything. And that awareness was of Gentry's voice as he argued with the sentry at the gate.

"You damn well will let me in! Stand back, Corporal! This woman's badly hurt."

Directly afterward she felt the animal go on at its plodding walk.

Chapter Three

There had been no more pressing reason for Caleb Ash accompanying Peebles's detail down the canyon to the scene of the massacre than for Mike Clears to go. His hardware goods were safe enough, since it was obvious no one would be traveling the road. Nor did the sight of bodies with or without scalps attract him; he had seen many dead, and the wanton killing of the Apaches always roused him to a rage. He would gladly have forgone the experience.

But one detail of Shotwell's story alarmed and sickened the big man. In addition to that he was utterly confused and he had decided quite suddenly it was all-important that he be one of the first to look over the wagons. So, to strengthen his reason for going, he told Peebles that someone who knew how to read sign should look around down there.

Ash had never been quite so physically sick as when he first glimpsed the bodies of the women. His face blanched to a pasty yellow tinge as he walked hurriedly away and in behind a tangle of alders. Afterward, he kept strictly away from the troopers loading the wagon Peebles had brought along. He took his time about circling the scene, ostensibly looking for sign. There was plenty of it, horse and moccasin tracks, but he paid it slight attention. He scarcely even noticed that the first two wagons were loaded with his hardware.

Finally he came across to stand with Peebles alongside the last Conestoga, the overturned one. Neither man had a thing to say as four troopers passed carrying a blanket-wrapped shape to the spring wagon. Peebles's expression was stern, his face almost as pale as Ash's.

A moment later Tim McCune came in with

four others carrying the last body. Approaching Peebles he glanced briefly at Ash with loathing and a wicked, obvious anger. Then, saluting smartly, he told Peebles, "We make the count only eleven, sir. Didn't Shotwell say there were twelve?"

Peebles frowned worriedly a moment. Then: "He was probably counting himself, Sergeant. Tell the men to take a five minute break before we start back."

McCune saluted again; and, as he turned and walked on down to join his men grouped by the horses near a clump of pines thirty yards below, Peebles was eyeing Ash with a faint smile. "Why's he got the chip on his shoulder?"

Ash's look was utterly grave as he answered, "Couple days ago I told him they should've hung Dan Gentry." Then, seeming to dismiss the matter as a trivial one hardly worth noticing, he glanced on up the road toward the other wagons, drawling, "It's a lucky thing for me those butchers were only after scalps and horses."

"Why, Caleb?"

"Usually they fire the wagons. If they'd done that I'd be out somewhere close to eighteen hundred dollars."

"Your hardware?"

The scout nodded soberly. "After this I lay

out my cash only when goods are delivered. It ought to be a freighter's risk to haul through this country."

"Then you are a lucky man," Peebles said. "You're sure about tomorrow morning being soon enough to make the haul up to town?"

Ash nodded. "Them red devils won't be back."

Peebles looked off toward the creek. "Think I'll get a drink," he said and started across toward the alders.

Ash was over the worst of his qualms and, satisfied at having carried a certain point nicely with Peebles, he stood now idly surveying the wreck of the wagon. It wasn't a pretty sight, yet it roused in the scout a stubborn rebellion that finally made him tell himself, *He'd probably have gone to freighting, set himself up in business against me.* And then he began wondering if he could salvage any of Tipton's belongings. He had his eye on the iron bedsteads particularly. And he liked the looks of a big open-lidded brass-bound chest half covered by the wagon's crumpled canvas.

He was noticing how the chest lay, half on its side, its lid hanging open and the top tray spilled out. Several dresses and embroidered petticoats hung over the tray's edge, and sight of these gave the scout an uneasy feeling, one of embarrassment that he should be prying. But just then his sharp eye picked out a neat row of letters and a small gold-filigree box packed tightly between some articles of clothing at the bottom of the chest; and his unsettling qualms died before a fresher curiosity.

There lay in this big man's nature an innate furtiveness rarely noticeable in the face of his blunt and hearty surface mannerisms. Now that quirk had its way with him as he glanced casually across at the others, first at the troopers gathered near the horses below, then at Peebles standing by the creek looking toward the far rim.

Having made sure that no one was watching him, Ash stepped over and with the toe of a moccasin pushed the shards of a broken mirror from their frame. He looked exactly as he intended he should, to be casually surveying the litter lying about him. But from where he now stood he could look directly down into the trunk.

He noted that the bundle of letters had been disturbed and that several lay loose on top of the others. One he could see plainly enough to read the *Mrs. Harry Tipton, Acequia Madre, Santa Fe, Terr. of New Mexico,* scrawled across its face. Ash recognized it as Harry Tipton's handwriting.

He took another short step that put him closer to the chest and he could see several other articles in the near corner. He gave a slight start at sight of one, a thinly-bound book with *Ledger* printed across its face. Directly on top of it lay another book, this one scarcely larger then his hand. Across its black cover, in gold gilt, ran the legend *Thoughts From Day To Day.*

There was no good reason why Ash shouldn't have reached down, picked up both the books and the gold box and looked at them. Still, he went at it a different way, one that was typical. He squatted on his heels and began sorting through a scattering of pots and pans lying near by, all the while edging closer to the chest. A seemingly incurious glance toward the men below showed him that no one was looking this way. So, deliberately and in the same way he would have reached into a stream to catch a sleeping trout, he dipped his hand into the chest.

The motion of his hand once it was out of sight became swift, sure. First of all he opened the box to discover that it contained some fine turquoise-set Navajo bracelets and necklaces made of silver. Next his fingers darted to the ledger, opening it. The pages he glimpsed were filled with figures and entries written in Harry Tipton's uncertain scrawl. Last of all he thumbed open the smaller black book. It was penned in a finer hand than Harry

Tipton's. He read three lines only . . . *no attachments here that would prevent our doing as my husband proposes. Yet I have reluctance to . . .*

He straightened now, a furtive glance toward the others showing him Peebles idling away from the stream bank in this direction. The sober set of Ash's broad face didn't betray any emotion whatsoever, though he sensed that the lieutenant's eye was on him. He stepped on around the chest now and squatted on his heels, knowing that the canvas hid all but his head and shoulders from Peebles's sight. Then his hand snaked quickly back into the chest again and he snatched the book and the ledger.

Had Caleb Ash glanced down at this moment he would have seen Faith Tipton's dress and the mass of the girl's golden hair fanned out beyond the chest's corner. Less than ten minutes ago Tim McCune, coming across here to lift the canvas and peer under it, had missed seeing Faith by an even narrower margin. He had, in fact, idly noticed a rumpled edge of her skirt and assumed that it was just another of the several dresses spilled from the trunk.

But Ash didn't look down now, didn't have to. He was idly watching Peebles approaching the wagon. And in another moment the lieutenant was asking from the far side, "Finding anything interesting, Caleb?"

"Just Tipton's possibles," Ash said innocently. He lazily came erect then, right hand to hip holding tight the folded ledger and book he had a moment ago thrust down inside his belt.

He stood with that side away from Peebles as he eyed the wagon's spilled goods and soberly shook his head. "For a fact, this is a damned shame. Everything Harry Tipton collected over a lifetime shot to hell — wife, daughter, everything. All there'll be to show for it is some fresh graves and a pile of junk not worth fifty dollars at the outside. Makes you think, eh?"

Peebles was young and impressionable, and his face took on a bleak look. "If Fitzhugh will only let me be in on the kill!" he breathed softly yet savagely. He stood a moment longer staring in an outraged way at the capsized wagon. Then he turned abruptly to call, "Sergeant, let's move!"

Ash was transferring the ledger and book to a hip pocket as Tim McCune's salty voice rang out over the breadth of the canyon, calling in his men who had strayed off toward the creek. "All right, you pore, tired soldiers! Stir your bones!"

Chapter Four

This had been a long, trying day for Major Robert Fitzhugh, and he had kept to his bed much later than was his habit in taking an afternoon nap. Shortly after four he had been wakened by the return of Peebles's detachment and had thought about getting up. But then he'd fallen into a deep, dreamless sleep. Now wakening to see the oncoming night deepening the grayish light at his window, he lay quietly, his breathing purposely even and shallow so as not to bring on a fit of coughing.

From time to time he could hear Mary's light step passing between the kitchen and main room of the cabin, and for some minutes his thoughts were wholly upon her in a reflective way that was tender and deeply satisfying. Mary had strangely become the core of almost everything he found pleasant in life lately. Weeks ago he had been both surprised and pleased at finding that Phil had chosen such a charming woman. Her arrival had quieted some rather vague misgivings in him, and he had concluded that it was an error in judgment to have remembered Phil as an unpredictable youth who was something of a weakling. Their six-year separation had quite evidently worked its change, had turned his son into a man he found himself extremely proud of. Mary, plus the circumstances surrounding Phil's death, were good evidence that he had a right to be proud of him.

He supposed that Mary was cooking their supper and he was grateful for her thoughtfulness. Lately it had become acutely embarrassing to appear each evening to eat with the officers of his command, knowing as he did that they were closely observing the failing of his health and growing more concerned about it. George Spires particularly had become a nuisance with his constant insistence that Fitzhugh apply for a lengthy leave and go East for treatment and possible retirement. Retirement was a purgatory the major had no intention of suffering of his own free will. The Army was his life and to leave it would only be signing his death warrant; of that he was very certain.

This hour, when dusk was laying its shroud over the jagged hills and evening's cool breeze brought strongly the scent of the pines, was the one he liked best of all the day. Now, wanting to take the last possible measure of enjoyment from it, he threw back the blankets and left his bed, holding to the headboard until the dizziness and unsteadiness that had lately been with him drained away.

Going to the window then he looked out across the shadowed parade and the uneven ranks of the foothills beyond to the deepening azure of the jagged western horizon, wondering if by this time tomorrow evening K Troop wouldn't be threading its way through the buttes and mesas of the broken country off there.

Everything depended on Washington, of course. At midday, on learning of the wagon-train massacre, he had sent a long message over the wire to Denver. This evening, having asked Caleb Ash to be here to give an opinion on what was to be expected of the renegades, he would send another emphasizing the urgency of immediate action. It might be only six or eight hours, but more likely a day or even two or three days before he would receive authorization to act in this situation.

The fact of his having been stripped of all independence of action, of having to consult Washington through the Department in Denver before making even the most minor disposition of his forces, rankled deeply and gave him a feeling of being shackled and at the mercy of the hostiles. But such developments were only to be expected after the disastrous outcome of Gentry's ambush last month. He was putting up with the situation as best he could.

Just now a harsh ring of voices sounding from the direction of the main gate broke the peacefulness and quiet of the moment, and Fitzhugh frowned in irritation. Perhaps it was because he'd just been thinking of Gentry that one of those voices seemed strangely like the man's, its tones deep and compelling. Only when he realized the absurdity of Gentry being on the post did the impression leave him and, his enjoyment of this interval completely gone, he turned from the window and began putting on his clothes.

He was still feeling that slight irritation a few minutes later when Mary knocked at his door; and his tone was impatient as he answered, "Yes?"

"It's Corporal Rawlins, Father. They want you at Headquarters."

"I'll be along presently." He had spoken harshly and was immediately regretting it. So when he shortly came out of his room to find Mary waiting by the porch door he crossed over to her with a smile and said apologetically, "Guess the sleep turned me sour, Mary."

She handed him his hat, the look in her dark eyes one of concern. "Couldn't someone else attend to whatever it is? You should be resting. And the dinner's almost ready."

"Then I'll hurry," he said. "I must hear what Ash has to say." And he went on out.

They were waiting for him on the Headquarters porch, Peebles and Ash and Captain Grell. And after he had taken his officers' salutes and said, "Good evening, gentlemen," it was Sam Grell who at once announced:

"Sir, we need your help."

Fitzhugh nodded, regarding his adjutant. And Grell went on lamely, "There's been — well, sir, a young woman was found alive down there at the wagons. She's been brought in to George Spires. She's hurt, how badly we don't know yet."

Fitzhugh's look was grave only a moment before it brightened. "It's unfortunate she's hurt, but how splendid she survived!" He glanced at Peebles. "You should have wakened me, let me know about it, Lieutenant."

"But I didn't bring her in, Major," Peebles said uncomfortably.

"Then who did?"

It was Grell who answered, saying awkwardly, "She was found late in the afternoon. It was — was Dan Gentry who found her. Lord knows how it happened to be him. But he's here right now down at George's cabin. It hasn't been ten minutes since he brought the girl in."

Fitzhugh's thin, sallow face tightened in an expression that showed no emotion whatsoever. He stood a moment in thought, then said

69

tonelessly, "And of course you're wondering what to do about him. Suppose you send Corporal Rawlins down and ask the doctor if he'll be good enough to come to my office."

Grell, vastly relieved, saluted and turned in the door.

And Fitzhugh said to the other two, "Let's go on in. I'm sure you have a lot to tell me."

They went on into the major's office, and Fitzhugh sat at his desk, asking the scout a question that started the big man talking. Once the major interrupted with a question, and when Ash finally went silent Fitzhugh was staring down at his desk in a brooding, considering way.

"We can at least be thankful they didn't get more of our horses this time," he said shortly, looking up at the scout and smiling faintly as he added, "You're about the only man I know who's profited from Sour Eye's forays, Mister Ash."

The scout's bronzed face took on a dark flush, and he said testily, "Could I help it if you needed remounts when Gentry lost all those animals?"

"Not at all, not at all," the major hastened to assure him. "I meant nothing personal." He was obviously surprised at Ash's touchiness and, deciding on the best way to put the man at his ease again, asked, "Then what's your opinion on what the 'Paches will do now?"

"Head south over the line, collect themselves some Mexican scalps and livestock, and try and hole up in those hills down there close to Cochise's people. It's what they did last time after they caught Gentry's detail and hid all those animals."

It was Fitzhugh's turn to be uneasy now. He straightened in his chair, trying to cover his annoyance over this second reference to something he had asked his officers not to mention in his presence, a fact Ash obviously wasn't aware of.

"Then I'll make my plans on your opinion, Caleb. We —"

His words broke off as the door opened. Doc Spires entered the room. The medico was a stooped slat of a man crowding old age, and now, meeting the major's glance his narrow face wore a dour expression. "I know what you're going to say," he stated bluntly, unceremoniously. "But it couldn't be helped. Dan had no choice."

"The woman," Fitzhugh said. "Is she badly injured?"

"A possible concussion. And naturally she's unstrung. But 'woman' is hardly the thing to call her. She's a downright beautiful young girl."

"Who is she?"

"Tipton's daughter, Faith by name."

"And how did Gentry happen to find her?"

"He was on his way out and stopped to look the wagons over. His animal shied, and he thought it queer and investigated. She was buried under something spilled from a wagon. Evidently took a hard blow when the thing went over. She was unconscious most of the day, till long after Dan found her."

Fitzhugh's look was relieved. "Then you think she'll be all right, George?" He waited for the medico's nod, went on, "Give her my compliments. And in view of your being a bachelor, why not move her to my place? There's the extra bed in Mary's room."

"I'll do that. And you might tell Mrs. Fitzhugh to keep a close eye on her tonight. She's got more downright guts than nine out of ten men. Hasn't broken down yet. But there's a limit to what anyone can stand. She may take a turn for the worse."

"Mary will watch her."

"Another thing," Spires said. "She's worried about the wagons. It seems her father owes money on the goods intended for Mike Clears and Ash here. If you could have Sam Grell see to the collection of it her mind would be relieved a —"

"Collection?" Caleb Ash cut in, his voice

72

such a growl that it startled them all. "Those goods're paid for!"

Fitzhugh frowned, glancing at Spires. And the medico told Ash, "I'm only repeating what she said."

Ash laughed harshly, his big voice filling the room. "She's got another think comin', Doc! That hardware's paid for and I can prove it."

Spires only shrugged. "Then that's that."

"Her father probably didn't discuss business matters with her," Fitzhugh remarked placatingly. "At any rate, let's wait till she's rested before we go on with the matter."

"Suits me," Ash drawled. "But no meddlin' woman's goin' to do me out of what's rightfully mine!"

Fitzhugh paid scant attention to the scout's salty words, so absorbed was he in deliberating something else now. They all sensed what it was and were nervously waiting for him to speak. At length he glanced up at Spires. "George, see that Gentry leaves at once. There's nothing more he can do now, and his being here makes it awkward for all of us. You can thank him for —" He caught himself, shaking his head. "No, not that. Just tell him to go."

On his way out Spires commented dryly, "He'll go afoot. That mare of his is done in.

She wasn't any good to begin with and she damn near killed herself carrying that load up here."

The door had barely closed behind the doctor when Ash was saying, "Suppose she sticks by her guns, Major? Does she just rob me blind?"

"How can she? You said you had proof."

"So I have. In writing. But —"

"Could Shotwell help us?" Peebles interrupted.

"Shotwell?" Fitzhugh asked.

"The teamster, the one that brought the news this noon, sir. He might be able to straighten us out on this."

Fitzhugh eyed Ash obliquely. "Do you want to find him and ask him about it?"

Ash's look was momentarily uncertain. But then in his bluff way he said, "Wouldn't hurt to try, would it? But it'll be you he talks to, not me. I know where I stand."

The major nodded. "Yes, that would be best." He glanced at his lieutenant. "Have the men eaten yet?"

"They're eating now, sir."

"Then as soon as they've finished send a man down to town and have him bring this man Shotwell up here to see me."

Ash had stepped across to the door. Opening it, he asked, "That's all you want of me, Major?"

"That's all. We'll be calling on you if any favorable word comes in over the wire."

The scout nodded and went on out across the adjoining room past the duty sergeant's desk and onto the porch. He paused there to take out a plug of tobacco and cut a wedge from the corner of it. As he tongued the chew from the clasp knife's thin, keen blade he was still feeling the shock that had hit him twenty minutes ago on first learning that Faith Tipton was still alive. Her being here threw his plans off, complicated them to a point where he wondered whether or not he dared carry through the deception he had so carefully thought out.

But then, thinking of Shotwell, his expression all at once changed from a worried one to a slowly-smiling one. Snapping shut the knife's big blade, he went quickly down the steps and out the graveled path to the rail where his bay was tied.

It was dark now, and he crossed the parade at a fast trot, heading for the main gate marked by the feeble glow of a lantern. The trooper on guard there heard him coming and stepped out from the sentry box with carbine slacked in the bend of his arm. At the last moment Ash realized he shouldn't appear to be hurrying and he tightened rein, and the bay was at a walk coming in on the gate.

75

Then he saw who the sentry was, and all his concern left him as he said affably, "How goes it, Johnny?" He brought his animal to a stand and without waiting for a reply said, "I hear Gentry's back again."

The trooper's look was rueful, angry. He shook his head. "Did the sergeant ever comb me over for lettin' him in!"

"Has he left yet?"

"Not yet."

Ash was smiling crookedly now. "How come you did it, Johnny? Changed your mind about him?"

"By God, no!" Corporal John Ewing's jaw set hard in indignation. Ash appeared unconvinced and his look made the trooper ask defensively, "What was I supposed to do? Here was this girl, blood all over her face and the captain —"

"You did all right, Johnny," Ash cut in mildly. "You always do all right."

The scout's words brought a look of apprehension, of wariness, to Ewing's narrow face. Stepping closer to the bay, Ewing looked furtively around before saying in a low, grating voice, "Caleb, I don't like the way things're shapin' up. Not a damn bit! McCune's been watchin' me. Every time I look around there he is starin' at me. This mornin' I braced him, asked him what the hell he's got on his mind.

He says to me, 'Maybe nothin', Johnny boy.' Then he just grins and walks off."

Ash shrugged with a nonchalance he was in no way feeling. "Forget McCune. What could he know?"

"Nothin'!" Ewing burst out in a hushed voice. "That's it. What is there he could know?"

He was about to add to that when suddenly he turned, listening to the rapid sound of hoof-strikes coming in along the bench road. He darted a glance at Ash, said, "I'll let you know if I find out anything," then stepped out to the center of the gate as a rider came in out of the shadows. "Halt!" he called.

"Easy, soldier. Easy!" Mike Clears walked his horse into the light toward the sentry box, toward Ash, asking unceremoniously, "Caleb, what's this I hear about a girl being found down there at those wagons? Was it really Gentry that brought her in?"

"So he did, Mike."

"Brought her here?"

The scout nodded. Then, catching a slur of sound from behind him along the parade, he turned in the saddle and looked off into the darkness. In another moment he was see-ing a man's tall shape followed by that of a horse coming toward him out of the shadows.

"Who was she?" Clears wanted to know.

"Here's your man," Ash drawled, knowing now that it must be Gentry who was approaching. "Let him tell you."

In a few seconds Gentry came on into the lantern's light leading the *grulla* mare. And Clears, seeing him, said, "That girl, Dan. Was it Tipton's daughter?"

Ewing was scowling now, and for a moment Gentry seemed to be gauging the strength of the man's animosity. But then he ignored the trooper and nodded to Clears. "Yes, it was Tipton's daughter." At once his glance swung up to Ash. It was agate-hard, and he said, "George Spires tells me your story and the girl's don't agree."

"They don't."

"You claim you paid Tipton?"

"I do," Ash stated, adding pointedly, "If it's any of your affair."

Gentry's eyes clung to the big man a deliberate moment before he looked at Clears again. "Mike, I'm leaving," he said. "For good this time. So maybe you'll do me a favor."

The exchange of words a moment ago had meant little to the saloonman, who now asked guardedly, "What kind of a favor?"

"Seeing that Ash pays the Tipton girl what was due her father."

It was the sudden outright startlement in

Mike Clears's eyes rather than anything he sensed himself that gave Gentry warning in that instant. He glanced quickly around to see Caleb Ash already dropping from the saddle toward him. He let go the mare's reins, lifted his arms, and tried to wheel out of the way.

But Ash was too fast. With a leap amazingly fast for a man so big he lunged at Gentry. All the weight of his massive upper body was in that first full swing of his knotted fist. It caught Gentry on the shoulder and knocked him backward and off his feet, hitting the ground so hard that he slid along it. Ash came on at him and, before he could roll away, kicked him savagely in the chest.

Had the scout been wearing boots the blow would have broken several of Gentry's ribs. As it was, Gentry's breath was driven from his lungs in a sharp groan. And as Mike Clears and Ewing watched in awe, Gentry somehow managed to roll clear of the swing of Ash's other foot and get his knees under him.

He saw Ash coming at him again and knew he didn't have time to get to his feet. So he drove his body forward in a diving roll that caught the scout at the knees and knocked his legs from under him. Ash went down clawing and kicking as Gentry scrambled out of the way.

This time Gentry was erect before Ash was

ready. Gentry had a fleeting thought of the gun riding his thigh, then at once forgot it. He stepped in on the bigger man as he was rising and threw two fast, hard uppercuts at his face. His left missed, but his right connected solidly with Ash's ear. The man was jolted hard, was badly hurt, and crossed his arms in front of his face, crouching down, backing away a step.

There was one exultant moment when Gentry knew he had decided this. He threw a long, full swing at Ash's chest, and the man's arms came down instinctively. Then Gentry hit with a vicious, full punch at the hinge of the jaw and connected solidly.

Ash was staggered; He stumbled unsteadily backward, nearly falling. But then as Gentry was following his advantage the scout gasped hoarsely, "Johnny!"

Ewing hesitated but an instant. Then he stepped in swinging his rifle club-fashion as Gentry was bracing himself to throw the blow he knew would be the last he would need.

It was then that Mike Clears cried sharply, "Dan! Watch it!"

The words were barely spoken when a stunning blow struck Gentry at the back of the head. His knees buckled, and he felt himself going down. He felt nothing as he hit the ground.

80

In that moment when he saw Gentry's right fist draw back to strike, Caleb Ash tensed his massive frame against the expected blow, knowing with a stunned and helpless certainty that he was beaten. The skull-aching impact of Gentry's knuckles against his ear and jaw had left him completely befuddled. His head was ringing, and he was only vaguely aware of Mike Clears's warning shout. He didn't know that his outcry to Ewing had even been heard until suddenly he saw the rifle butt arcing down, saw Gentry collapse in a loose sprawl.

Afterward he stood unsteadily, feet spread wide, staring down dully in disbelief at the unconscious Gentry while he dragged in deep lungfuls of air into his aching chest. Gentry's solid punches had really hurt him, and his senses were so numbed that it was several seconds before he became aware of Mike Clears's voice raised in anger.

When he did finally look up it was to see Johnny Ewing, standing over Gentry, grudgingly lowering his rifle and taking a backward step. Mike Clears stood beside his horse directly beyond. There was a .45 Colt's in the saloonman's hand, and it was pointed squarely at the trooper.

"Back, I tell you!" Clears said flatly now. And Ewing moved farther from Gentry.

Ash hardly cared what was happening between these two. He shook his head to clear it and then plodded unsteadily across to the bay, climbing awkwardly astride the animal. He was feeling an acute shame at these two having witnessed the thrashing he had taken and wanted nothing so much as to get away from here now. He lifted rein and rode on past Mike Clears, a furtive sideward glance letting him see the scornful, derisive look that was directed up at him.

Anger boiled furiously in him then, and he took the bay away at a run. Only when he had gone on a hundred yards did he look back to see Ewing and Clears together lifting Gentry's limp bulk across the *grulla's* saddle.

The night's chill air soon sobered Ash, and by the time he was down off the bench and had reached his corral at the street's upper end he was once more considering what he'd had in mind before meeting Gentry. And now a heady excitement took the place of his resentment as he turned the roan into the corral. Shortly he walked off across his wide, cluttered yard to his shack opposite the new building on the far side of the gate.

Some ten minutes later he was standing at the back corner of Mike Clears's bunk barn far down the street, eyeing the darkness along the alley to make sure he was alone. It was important that no one should see him, for he was playing some long odds in having come here to find Shotwell and talk with him before the Army got to him. All he had to go on was what Peebles had said on their way down the canyon at midday, that Shotwell was dead beat, that he'd come across here after seeing Mike Clears, that he'd probably sleep for a week.

This was the same kind of gamble Ash had already played twice today, ever since making sure that Shotwell was the wagon train's only survivor and realizing how extremely simple it would be to carry through his long-planned claim of ownership of his hardware. First, he had taken the ledger from Tipton's trunk as self-protection; the diary was merely something that had roused his curiosity and he hadn't yet looked into it. Secondly, he had made his flat claim there in Fitzhugh's office regardless of the girl.

Faith Tipton's unexpected appearance plus her knowing the truth about his not having paid for the goods had thrown his calculations off balance. But so tempting was this chance for laying his hands on so much easy money that he had brazenly and stubbornly held to his original plan of claiming the goods. What he intended doing now was his gamble on making good that claim.

Peering up at the top of the log wall above him, he was remembering the arrangement of the inside of the barn. A stovepipe elbowing out between the logs and rising above the line of the peaked canvas roof told him that this was the corner he wanted to climb. Once he had decided that he stepped up onto a log-end three feet above the ground and started up the eight-foot wall. And presently he was sitting astride the butt of the topmost log and reaching over to cut the rope that tied the canvas to it.

He lifted the canvas slightly and went belly-down on the log, pushing head and shoulders inside. He peered down into the thick shadows, making out a potbellied stove in this near corner directly below and the long rows of double bunks beyond. The barn's interior was dimly lighted by a hooded lantern hanging on the log upright that supported the canvas roof's long ridgepole. Up at the street door a second lantern hung over the makeshift counter, behind which sat Sims, Clears's man who ran the place. Sims was there dozing in his chair. Noises from the street blended with those of the big room — snores, heavy breathing, the grunt of a man turning in his bunk. The sound Ash made as he hung by his hands and then dropped to the dirt floor was drowned by the others. Squatting down so that he could peer between the bunks, he saw that Sims at his desk hadn't stirred.

There was no furtiveness in the way he set about finding Shotwell, though he walked as quietly as a stalking mountain cat. He stood erect and moved slowly, peering at the feebly lit faces in the bunks. Seeing him moving this way between the beds, no onlooker would have been even mildly curious.

Luck was with him. He found Shotwell in a bottom bunk, the next to the end one of the row that ran on back to the stove-corner. Ash knelt silently alongside the man and reached out and put a hand over his mouth.

Shotwell's eyes came wide open. Quickly, Ash bent over and whispered with his mouth close to the man's ear. "Nothing's wrong, friend. Just want to talk with you. Remember me? I was with the soldiers this morning."

Shotwell nodded and tried to move his head around. But Ash kept his hand tight over the teamster's mouth, hastily whispering, "Leave your boots here and come on over behind the stove. I'll be there." And he straightened and walked away toward the stove-corner.

It was a long quarter-minute before the bunk creaked and Shotwell's spare shape came erect in the aisle between the bunks; and in that interval Ash's nerves drew taut, and perspiration began to stand out on his forehead at the likelihood of Shotwell's balking.

The teamster approached the stove warily, stopping well out of Ash's reach. "What d'you want?" his tone was suspicious, too loud.

"Couple of things," Ash replied in a harsh whisper. "But let's be quiet about it. Did you know they found a girl alive in the wagons?"

"No!" the teamster breathed incredulously. "Which one?"

It was a moment before Ash could take this in and ask over his surprise, "Was there more than one?"

"Sure. Faith and Laura. But o' course it couldn't be Laura. I seen her scalped with my own eyes."

"Who was Laura?" Ash asked warily.

"A young girl we brought on from Santa Fe. Nice. Pretty, too, and a help to Tipton's women. She paid Tipton to bring her this far. She'd heard how maybe she could travel west with the paymaster from the fort his next trip. She was tryin' to get to 'Frisco. Her father's out there."

"Let's talk quieter!" Ash said urgently, thinking of what the teamster had told him. "Anyway, this was Harry Tipton's daughter they found. How come you didn't mention the other one this mornin'? All you mentioned was women bein' along."

"Was there any reason to name 'em?" Shotwell asked testily.

"No, no reason," Ash admitted placatingly.

"Faith Tipton alive!" Shotwell said then. "Well, something good had to come of this. She's the salt of the earth."

"That may be," Ash said guardedly, "but she's brought me a headache."

"How come?"

"Remember me askin' you this mornin' about my hardware?" Ash waited for the other's nod, went on. "Well, damn me if this girl don't claim the goods belong to her father, not me. And here I paid Harry eighteen hundred in gold, sent the money to him by express not eight weeks ago."

Shotwell stood silent a moment. "What's this got to do with me?"

"Everything. I'm hopin' you can back me up. Didn't Harry ever mention the stuff was paid for?"

"To me? Why should he?"

Ash cursed soundly, softly now, saying in a baffled way, "This sure puts me in a fix! So that's all you can tell 'em, is it? They're sending down for you tonight, pretty soon now."

"Who's 'they'?"

"The major up there at the fort. He was hopin' you could settle the thing."

The teamster shook his head. "Not me."

Ash stepped closer to him then, saying in a hushed way, "But you could settle it."

"How?"

Instead of answering, Ash drew from his pocket something he had a quarter-hour ago taken from beneath a loose board in the floor of his shack. He held it out in his hand.

The teamster kept his hands at his sides, asking suspiciously, "What is it?"

"Money. Gold! An even hundred."

"What for?"

"For you to say Tipton told you those goods were paid for when they ask you tonight."

Shotwell's jaw sagged open. Then he laughed softly, derisively. "Lie for you? Hunh-uh, mister! You don't pull a trick like that on the girl!"

"But it's no trick, I tell you!" Ash whispered harshly. "You come around to my place in the morning and I'll show you a receipt for that money signed by Harry Tipton. All I want is to get this thing settled. You can end it."

"Sure, but I won't."

Ash grunted his disgust, lowered his hand. "Then you want to stay on here as a witness while I take it to court?"

"Me stay on?" Shotwell chuckled. "Brother, I'm leavin' this town just as fast as I can get! Me for back East. I've freighted my last load through this God-forgotten country!"

"You think the Army'll let you go?" the scout insisted. "Did you ever see the Army get its teeth into a thing? You'll be here weeks, months, maybe, while they're writin' Denver provin' my claim."

Shotwell had nothing to say to that, and Ash in the faint light thought he saw a worried look come to the man's face. So he went on. "Look, Shotwell. It'll all come out the same in the end anyway. Those are my goods by law. All I'm tryin' to do is save us all trouble. Take this hundred and tomorrow you can leave here for good. I'll even throw in any horse you want to pick from my string. Or, if you'd rather, wait'll this Apache scare dies down and I'll send you across to Santa Fe as boss of my first wagons that pull out. Now how about that?"

Before Shotwell had the time to answer there were heavy steps along the front of the room by the street door and a voice up there was plainly heard to ask, "Sims, is that teamster still here? The one off that wagon train?"

And Sim's answer came just as plainly: "Far as I know. Why?"

"The major wants to see him. Right away."

"But he's paid up till four in the morning."

"He can come back."

Ash reached out and took a tight hold on

89

Shotwell's arm, breathing urgently, "Here's the hundred! Do you take it or do you loaf around here till the Army settles this?"

"Just what do I say?" Shotwell asked uncertainly.

"Tell the major you heard Tipton say I'd paid for the hardware. Just that. Tell him Tipton said it more than once." Ash's whispered words were urgent as he added hastily, "When you get back down here come straight and tell me how it went. My layout's that barn lot up the street. I'll be in the shack by the gate."

They could hear Sims now as he worked his way slowly along between the bunks at the front of the room. All at once Shotwell lifted a hand. "All right, give it here!"

Ash silently palmed the coins into the teamster's hand, saying quickly, "Get back to bed!" and Shotwell at once moved away into the shadows.

Ash was crouched behind the stove when Sims finally found his man, roughly shook the teamster, and told him to get up. Shotwell made a good pretense of being hard to waken and then complained bitterly about having to go out. But shortly he followed Sims up the aisle carrying his boots. While the trooper who had come down from the fort was explaining to Shotwell what was wanted of him, Ash was

90

on his way out over the log wall.

Later, in his shack at the stable yard, Caleb Ash hung blankets over the two windows before lighting the lamp sitting on the long packing-box he used for a desk. The room was bare of everything but the box, two caboose chairs, a hogsback stove and Ash's bed, covered with rumpled and dirty blankets.

Ash knelt now and moved the foot of the bed out from the wall. Then he pried loose a board the bed's near leg had been resting on and, reaching in under the floor, drew out Tipton's bent ledger, Mrs. Tipton's diary, and a soiled and stamped envelope.

He took these things over to his desk and sat down. Then he drew two sheets of paper from the envelope, which was addressed to him in Harry Tipton's hand and bore a Denver postmark. For some minutes he compared the signatures on the two sheets, one of which was genuine, the other a forgery he had accomplished after a vast amount of practice.

Finally satisfied that the signatures closely resembled each other, he returned the sheets to the envelope, laid it aside and began examining the ledger. Ten minutes later, after having read every entry, he knew that nothing in the book would affect his fortunes one way or another. He pushed it away from him then and began reading Mrs. Tipton's diary.

It took him twenty minutes to get through the book and when he had finished the last page he thumbed back through the others, folding the corners on four. Then, drawing his clasp knife, he carefully cut out those four pages.

Finally he took the ledger, envelopes, diary, and the clipped pages across the room and returned them to the hiding-place under the floor. He moved the bed back in place. He stood up then and stretched and yawned and afterward idled on back to the desk.

He was thinking of Shotwell now, wishing the man would show up. He sat behind the packing-box and leaned down to rummage in under its lid along one of the shelves he'd built there. Shortly he found what he was looking for, a grimy deck of cards. Then, lounging back in the chair, he began shuffling them, cutting them, dealing one card after another all the way through the deck. His stubby fingers were remarkably supple, and there was no break in their rapid movement between a deal off the top of the deck or off the bottom.

He went on doing that, just playing, just killing time.

Chapter Five

Mike Clears was at first convinced that Gentry must be seriously injured. His impulse had been to take Gentry on to George Spires. But then, judging from Johnny Ewing's manner that the feeling on the post was violently against Gentry, he decided to take him on down to town.

When he dismounted in the alley behind the *Lucky Find* and walked on back to the mare, he was encouraged at finding Gentry's breathing deep and even. He tied both animals and went on in for help.

It was old Ben Qualls he brought out with him and Qualls, not prepared for this, drew back in surprise when he saw who it was roped to the *grulla*.

"Him again?" he asked. "I thought he'd gone."

"So did I. Come on. Lend a hand." Clears was unknotting the rope.

"Why you botherin' with him, Mike?" the oldster asked in his caustic way.

"Never you mind. Get busy."

Qualls muttered his contempt for Gentry

and grudgingly helped Clears lift him down and carry him on into the office. Then the saloonman told him, "Hang around the door in there, Ben. I don't want anyone coming in on us."

"Wouldn't think you would," was the other's dry rejoinder as he went on into the saloon.

Clears's office was big and comfortable, ranging all the rear width of the building except for the space taken up by a small storeroom to the north. His walnut desk sat in the inside corner and was flanked by a window looking down-canyon to the south. Under the alley window was a broad rawhide-upholstered settee, and it was here that he and Qualls had laid Gentry. Beyond the alley door, at the foot of a steep and crude stairway climbing to Clears's bedroom above, a deer's head with a huge span of antlers stared sightlessly across toward the desk. Below the head hung a deer-leg gunrack holding two shotguns and a rifle. A grizzly's skin, an enormous one, lay across the floor with the head under the edge of a table occupying the outside corner between the two windows where the stove sat in wintertime. Clears had relative privacy here, for he had purposely built the door leading to his saloon of thick planks that shut out most of the noise.

Now as he began working over Gentry, trying to bring him around and not succeeding, he was really worrying, blaming himself for not having gone straight to George Spires regardless of the consequences. Bathing Gentry's face, even slapping it a few times, had no visible effect on the unconscious man. Presently Clears climbed the stairway to his snug sleeping-quarters under the building's roof-peak and came down with a bottle of spirits of camphor. When he held the uncorked bottle under Gentry's nose the unconscious man's breathing shortened. But that was all.

So Clears began rubbing Gentry's arms and legs, massaging the back of his neck. Several times he looked at his watch, the passage of time alarming him. He had been in the office thirty-five minutes when he finally went out to the bar and brought back a glass tumbler full of whisky. He managed to prop up Gentry's head and shoulders and force some of the raw liquor into his mouth.

At first he couldn't get Gentry to swallow. So he stretched him out flat again. At the next try Gentry gagged on the liquid, coughed. Then suddenly his long frame doubled up, he rolled onto his side, and his eyes came open. He struggled to get an elbow under him and then lay there with head hung, gagging and reaching for a full breath.

Clears had been kneeling alongside the settee. He got up wearily now and stepped over to the desk and set the glass on it. Then he leaned back against the desk's edge eyeing Gentry soberly, speculatively, feeling vastly relieved as Gentry shifted around, dropped his feet to the floor, and sat holding his head in his hands.

Abruptly Gentry spoke. "Why did you clip me, Mike? Just when I had him!"

"It was Ewing, not me."

Gentry's head came up, and their glances met. "How did I get here?"

"I brought you. Ewing would have brained you."

Gentry ran his hands gingerly along the back of his head and when he looked up again the pain, both physical and mental, betrayed itself in a feverish look in his dark eyes. "Don't know why you bothered, Mike. But you have my thanks."

Clears stood staring down gravely at him. "You'd better be heading out as soon as you feel like it."

Gentry nodded. But then he thought of something that made him ask, "And what about the girl?"

"What about her?"

"Just before Ash jumped me I'd asked you to do me — her a favor."

The saloonman frowned. "She's not my lookout."

"But Ash is trying to get away with something, Mike. She doesn't have a soul to help her."

"Suppose she doesn't? She means nothing to you. Or to me."

There was a faint scorn in Gentry's glance as it clung briefly to the saloonman's face and then dropped to the desk. He saw the half-full whisky glass, stood up, and came across to get it. He tilted it to his mouth, drained it.

Watching this, Clears asked, "More?"

Gentry nodded, handed over the glass, and Clears went on out with it. As Clears passed Ben Qualls in the barroom beyond the door the oldster asked, "Still out?"

"No. He's coming around."

"That's a shame," Qualls said feelingly, really meaning it.

Clears went on in behind his bar, filled the glass, and came back to the door again. He eyed his man obliquely, saying in a musing way, "I don't know what to think, Ben. I just don't."

"By God, I do!"

The saloonman shrugged and stepped on into the office. On the point of closing the door he went motionless. The room was empty. The alley door stood open.

He went quickly across there and out onto the back platform. The *grulla* stood as he had left her, tied to the rail, head hanging in weariness. The blackness along the alley showed him nothing. He called sharply, "Dan!"

The stillness out there remained unbroken, and finally, after listening for a brief interval, Clears went on back in and over to his desk. As he sank tiredly into the chair there he was becoming really worried, thinking back on Ben Quall's attitude toward Gentry. Nine out of ten people in the town who knew Gentry would feel the same as Ben had; and if Gentry was seen, there was no telling what would happen.

Yet, despite his worry, Clears was feeling a gloating satisfaction over the thorough mauling Gentry had given Ash up there by the post gate. He had never quite trusted Ash. He didn't like the man's too-positive heartiness and the way he had taken advantage of the circumstances here in demanding, and getting, outrageous prices for horses and his freighting services. Clears himself was doing business on a fair basis, sensing that when this boom quieted down he would keep his trade where the money-grubbers like Ash would fast lose theirs.

But now he forgot Ash in trying to see through the enigma of Gentry's behavior. He didn't understand Gentry's hasty disappearance but sensed that his own refusal to meddle in the Tipton girl's affairs might be the direct cause of it. He was regretting the stand he'd taken on that, for he knew he had already decided to do what he could to help Faith Tipton and had argued with Gentry out of sheer contrariness.

How long he sat there pondering those difficulties he had no way of knowing. It might have been twenty minutes, even a half hour. But the end of that interval was punctuated by the sound of a solid tread mounting the platform steps from the alley.

It was Dan Gentry, who came on in and slumped down on the settee. Something had gone out of the man and, noticing that, Clears said brusquely, "You're in no shape to travel. Better wait till morning."

Gentry gave no indication of having heard, instead saying lifelessly, "Couldn't find him."

"Who?"

"Shotwell. That teamster of Tipton's McCune had in here today."

Clears frowned. "What about Shotwell?"

Gentry looked across at him vacantly. "He might be able to help the girl. Tipton might have told him." Abruptly his glance took on life. "Mike, you've got to find him and see what he knows."

Clears understood now and nodded. "All right, I'll do what I can. But you turn in. Go on across there to the cave. Give the mare some grain and then get some sleep. No one'll bother you and you can head on out in the morning."

"That's a promise? About the girl?"

"I said I'll do what I can."

The way Gentry got up and walked to the door and out into the night without another word made Clears at once regret the uncalled-for irritation and gruffness he had put in his last words. It was a painful thing for him to witness a quality in Gentry that made the man look almost beaten, humbled to a far greater degree now than he had been at noon when he had been carrying the even heavier burden of his own troubles. And the saloonman half-way understood then what an added shock and strain these past few hours had put on Gentry. A man could stand so much and he marveled now that Gentry hadn't broken under the mental and physical beating this long day had given him.

Usually at this hour of the night Mike Clears would go out into the saloon and have a glass or two with his customers, do his only drinking of the day. But tonight he had no appetite for either liquor or company; and for a good half hour he sat on at his desk, thinking of

Gentry and growing more puzzled than ever about the man. The contradictions he saw in Gentry's actions today as opposed to the findings of the courts-martial were enormous, beyond his comprehension. And gradually the conviction came that he would have no peace of mind until he understood them.

Mike Clears's nature was a strongly speculative one, and as he considered what he knew of Gentry his impression strengthened that he was annoyingly close to discovering something that lay just beyond his grasp. He didn't know what it was; but something was there, something that would explain Gentry's inconsistencies.

It was this certainty that finally straightened him in his chair to call loudly, "Ben!"

Qualls opened the door and at a nod from Clears came on in. Then the saloonman was asking, "How long since you took a day off, Ben?"

The oldster lifted his bony shoulders. "Can't remember. Why?"

Clears's look was thoughtful and, staring down at the desk, he said with a trace of absent-mindedness, "You could be across at the agency by sunup."

"If I wanted to be there."

"Pack along enough grub to last you two or three days," Clears went on, ignoring the remark. "I want you to go to the ones you can trust, Ben. Men like Cut Nose and Bird Claw. Find out everything — every blessed thing, mind you — that they know about that tangle with Gentry's detail in the canyon. They usually —"

"Boss, you gone loco? Forget that sidewinder! Or go up to the fort and read what they wrote about his trial. They got it all down in black and white."

"I know." Clears's tone was so impatient that it at once overruled the other's protest. "What I'm after are the things that didn't come out at the trial."

"Like what?"

"If I knew what they were, I wouldn't be sending you. Get everything you can, the whole story. What men Sour Eye finished off himself, why they didn't kill Gentry and Tim McCune. And what did they think of young Fitzhugh as a scrapper? Get your friends to talking. They know plenty. Every other time those wild bucks have busted out the others have known every move they made."

Qualls shook his head in unfeigned disgust. "Suppose they're off on a hunt?" he argued.

"Then chase 'em down. Take as much time as you need."

"What if they won't talk?"

Mike Clears smiled faintly. "It's no use trying to get out of it, Ben. I want to know about this, and you're the only man who can get what I want. Those Apaches stole you from your folks, then turned around and raised you like one of their own. You know them like no white man alive. There isn't —"

His head swung around and he stopped speaking as the door's latch clicked and the door opened. The man who stood there was heavy-bodied and middle-aged. His ruddy face wore a worried cast as he asked, "Got a minute, Mike?"

"Come in, Ralph." Clears nodded to Qualls then, saying, "That's all, Ben. Don't waste any time but stay long enough to get all there is to get."

Ben Qualls edged on past the newcomer and was muttering as he went out.

"How's Sarah, Ralph?" Clears asked after the door had slammed.

"Fine. Got her new room nearly finished for her." Ralph Blake, who ran a butcher shop up the street, was just as obviously stalling for time as his look was uncomfortable, almost embarrassed.

Clears detected this strangeness in the man's behavior at almost the exact instant he noticed the tarnished nickeled shield pinned to Blake's vest pocket. And now, grinning broadly, the saloonman asked, "Is this an official call, Ralph?"

"For a fact, it is." Blake glanced down guiltily at the deputy sheriff's badge he so seldom wore. His duties as a law officer were so meager that he took a lot of ribbing over the fifteen dollars the sheriff's office in Santa Fe sent him each month. It was a standing joke in the fast-growing community that he was too mild-mannered and shy to be a peace officer, that he nicely avoided trouble on the theory that most such difficulties resolved themselves. The fact that Blake was flaunting his badge tonight was an ominous sign to Clears, though he didn't show his awareness of that.

Clears decided now to let the other do the talking, and after a short silence the deputy blurted out, "Now don't get sore, Mike. But they say you been seen a couple times today in his company. So maybe you can help me."

"Who've I been seen with?"

"This Captain Gentry."

Wariness touched Clears's glance as he drawled, "What about him?"

"He's been combin' the town tonight lookin' for that fella that got away from them wagons down-canyon. Sims across the way says he was there and he was at Belle's place and a couple more. One of them Swedes from placers tangled with him when he come into Jake's restaurant. Named him for what he is.

Gentry swung on him, busted in a couple of his teeth."

"If you're making arrests on that count you'd have half the town in the lockup inside a week, Ralph."

Blake shook his head vehemently. "But that ain't it! It's about Shotwell. Y'see, Gentry caught up with him."

"He did?" Clears sat straighter in his chair.

"He did," Blake echoed solemnly. "A man from up the canyon just found Shotwell lyin' in the creek with his head under water. His skull's busted open like a melon. If you can tell me where this Gentry is, I'll do my damnedest to arrest him and get him on out to the sheriff before they string him up."

Mike Clears sat dumbfounded, too stunned to utter a word as his panicked thinking tried to take all this in. And as though this moment had been reserved particularly as one to confound him utterly, he now caught the mutter of angry voices sounding from the saloon and knew that Ralph Blake hadn't come here alone. The crowd out there knew about Shotwell, about Gentry. It had the makings of a mob.

Suddenly and without a trace of doubt Mike Clears knew that Dan Gentry could never have done this thing.

He came up out of the chair now, his jaw

set in anger as he fixed the deputy with a scornful stare. "That's a fine theory, Ralph. It might hold water if I didn't know how wrong it was."

Blake asked testily, "What's wrong with it?"

"Just this. I know Gentry was out looking for Shotwell. I know because I followed him, tagged right along behind him while he stopped at all those places you mention. When he clipped that Swede at Jake's I was looking through the window and nearly bought into the scrap. But Gentry cleared out, and afterward I brought him back here. How long ago was it they found Shotwell?"

Blake stirred out of his surprise to answer, "Twenty minutes or so."

Clears shook his head now and deliberately added to his bald lie. "You're barking up the wrong tree. Gentry left here maybe five minutes before you walked in." He nodded down to the glass on the desk. "We had a long talk and some drinks. He hasn't been out of my sight all evening."

The deputy's face took on color. "How come you're stickin' up for that no-account, Mike?"

"Why shouldn't I? Dan Gentry's my friend." There was a strong lift of pride in Clears as he made the statement. And he had the feeling that this somehow made up for his never having spoken one word in Gentry's defense over the long weeks since the beginning of the man's trouble.

Ralph Blake sighed in a baffled way. "You can say that after what he's done?"

"I damn well can! Do you walk out on a man when his luck's gone back on him?"

"But, Godamighty, he's —"

Clears waved the man to silence. "We won't argue that. You came here with your mind made up to something that isn't so. Now get on out there and tell those people how wrong you were."

Blake stared helplessly at the door, listening to all the voices out there. He looked at the saloonman. "Mike, you got to do it for me! These folks think the sun rises and sets right out of your vest pocket. Me, I'm just something they laugh at every time I pin on this damned badge."

Mike Clears shook his head. "You started it, you finish it."

"But what'll I tell 'em?"

"Just what I told you. This afternoon I loaned Gentry a horse so he could leave. You know what happened, why he had to come back. He was trying to help that Tipton girl when he went looking for Shotwell. He had nothing against the man, absolutely nothing. I'd made up my mind he was to get out of here without any more trouble. So I stayed with him the whole evening. He couldn't have killed Shotwell even if he'd had a reason."

"Suppose they won't believe me?"

"They will."

The deputy stepped hesitantly to the door now. Before he went out he squared his shoulders and stood straighter.

Once the door had closed Mike Clears went across there and stood with his ear close to the panel, listening. He heard the solid thump of some heavy object being pounded against the bar. Most of the loud talk died away. Then Ralph Blake's voice rose over the others that hadn't quieted. Clears couldn't distinguish the deputy's words but the man's tone was surprisingly forceful. Once another voice interrupted, and Blake answered tersely, evidently convincingly, for afterward the room gave out its normal sounds, and there was the continuous dull thumping of the swing-doors up front, evidence of a heavy traffic Mike Clears hoped was on its way out.

When he at length turned out across the office again, the saloonman mopped his damp forehead and was surprised to find that his hand was shaking. He took up the full glass of whisky from the desk and emptied it in long swallows that left him gagging for breath but feeling steadier.

This had been a close thing, and Clears was feeling the strain now. He had no regrets, nor was there a moment's question over what he had done. This much he owed Dan Gentry. He felt a cleaner and a better man. All these weeks he had stood idly by, saying nothing, doing nothing in Gentry's defense. Now he had said something, done something.

He was tired, sleepy, and for a long moment he stood there eyeing the narrow stairway that climbed the far wall to his living-quarters above. But then, reaching a sudden decision, he stepped across to lift down one of the double-barreled shotguns from its wall bracket. In one of the desk drawers he found some brass loads of buckshot. He loaded the weapon and dropped some spare shells in his coat pocket. Then he went out across the alley, down across the footbridge, and started up the road to the cave.

He was breathing heavily when he reached the cave mouth and he paused there to get his breath and look out across the town. He neither heard nor saw anything to make him uneasy and he briefly considered going back down to the *Lucky Find*, almost giving up the idea that had brought him up here. But then finally he walked on into the cave.

He knew every square foot of this place and made his way surely on back past the horse stalls in the pitch-dark until he knew he stood close to the haystack. He stopped, lit a match, and saw Gentry lying sprawled and asleep within ten feet of him. He shook the match out and went across there, kneeling and shaking Gentry by the shoulder.

"Got something to tell you, Dan," he said when he felt Gentry stir. "Better sit up and listen."

He heard Gentry move and began talking then. Briefly, but omitting nothing, he told about Shotwell's death and the visit Blake had paid him. Finished, he laid the shotgun across Gentry's lap, telling him, "This is just in case. It's loaded. Here are some extra shells." And he took the loads from his pocket and handed them across.

He was rising when Gentry said quietly, "I could be the one they're after. How did you know that —"

"You damn well aren't the one!" Clears cut in. "That's all that matters. Now get back to sleep."

He had started back toward the cave mouth when Gentry asked soberly, "Why did you do it, Mike?"

Clears halted, asking incredulously, "You think I did it?"

"No, not that. Why did you lie for me?"

As his startlement drained away Clears answered querulously, "How would I know? Does a man have to explain everything he does?" And he walked on away.

"You're a queer cuss, Mike."

The saloonman barely caught those words. He chuckled softly, what Gentry had said pleasing him far more than would any further word of thanks.

Chapter Six

Dawn was only a thinning of night's blackness to a weak gray light that cast no shadows, and soon a steady drizzle blanketed Sentinel's lofty peak. As the rain swept slowly down across the craggy timbered slopes, finally to shroud both fort and town, Lieutenant Peebles started down-canyon with his detail heading for the wagons. Caleb Ash and a crew of men and horses joined the column at the foot of the bench road.

It wasn't many more minutes before four troopers were hauling the new pine coffins from the post's hump-roofed forage shed across to the burial ground at the isolated northeast corner of the palisade. There the troopers lined the coffins in front of the freshly dug graves that would soon match eighteen other slowly settling mounds near by. By the time the funeral party arrived, the warps in the coffin lids were puddled with the rain.

The service was informal, brief. Mary Fitzhugh had driven the buggy close to the open graves. And while the major spoke his words, reading first from the Scriptures, she stood with her arm about Faith Tipton's slender waist, holding an umbrella in the other hand. She was more worried about Fitzhugh than she was about Faith, for the girl had displayed such unmistakable determination and fortitude in insisting on coming out here that Mary felt somehow cheated in the lack of any need for comforting her.

There was a dignity about Robert Fitzhugh that stood out magnificently at times like this, and it was perhaps because of his uneffusive sincerity that Faith remained calm, giving no outward sign of much emotion. That stolidity seemed strange to Mary; or rather it did until she stole a sideward glance at Faith's delicate profile and saw her cheeks glistening and her blue eyes brimming with tears. In that moment Mary tightened her arm, and the grateful and grief-stricken glance Faith gave her brought her own tears in a flood.

Afterward, when they were back in the cabin and Mary had kindled the logs in the stone fireplace, they sat out a long uncomfortable silence staring into the fire. Finally Mary, embarrassed by it, went into the kitchen to feed the stove and heat the coffee left over from breakfast.

It was when Mary brought the coffee in and was pouring it that Faith broke the long silence by saying musingly, "Dad was a soldier once. He was with Lee till the end of the War. I have the feeling that he isn't so alone out there, so close to those others and with Mother beside him."

Mary nodded sympathetically, and after another moment Faith went on, "Those other graves, Mary. There were so many new ones. Why?"

It took Mary several seconds to think out an answer. "Those men were lost seven weeks ago against the Apaches," she said quietly. "My husband was one of them."

Faith's look was at once startled and contrite. "Oh, I'm so sorry! I should have known better than to ask."

"But I don't mind your asking." Mary eased the awkwardness by passing Faith her cup, adding lightly, "I do hope this rain won't last all day, though we need it badly."

Faith sipped her coffee, and once again there was a weighty silence. Then abruptly Faith was saying, "Forgive me for asking one more thing, Mary. But when — when you lost your husband, had that anything to do with Captain Gentry? He's — well, in disgrace, isn't he?"

Mary said cautiously, "I'm afraid he is."

"Do you mind very much telling me about it?" Faith asked hesitantly. "The doctor only put me off when I asked him. Am I being unkind?"

"Not at all, Faith." Mary turned to put her cup on the table at her elbow. "It's a mixed-up story, really. You wouldn't understand it unless you know what had gone on before. To begin with, I still like and admire Dan Gentry."

"So do I."

Faith's spontaneous agreement roused a twinge of jealousy in Mary, the absurdity of it making her smile inwardly. "It goes back to Gentry's dislike for a man down below in town, Caleb Ash," she said then. "For some time Captain Gentry had questioned this Ash's right to demand such high prices for the horses he furnished the garrison here. He —"

"I happen to know about Ash," Faith cut in. Then she caught herself, saying, "Excuse me. Do go on."

Mary was noticing the way the damp weather had tightened the curl of Faith's high-piled golden hair and now enviously wished her own could be coaxed to take on even the semblance of a wave as she said, "Dan — Captain Gentry had tried to convince the major that it would be worth the effort sending men down to Fort Starke. To bring in remounts from there, where they can be bought cheaper. But the major never felt justified in weakening his strength here, sparing the men to make the trip. Then finally Ash tried again to raise his prices. Even the major saw that a stop must be put to it."

As Mary hesitated, Faith asked, "That's what they finally did, went to Fort Starke?"

"Yes. Things were quiet among the Indians. And Gentry had worked out a plan for the men leaving here secretly on several successive nights, riding by twos and threes so as not to rouse any curiosity. It was hoped that no one would discover they had gone. Phil — my husband, left with Gentry and his sergeant one midnight."

"Was that a mistake? Were the men lost because they weren't together?"

"No. They all arrived safely at Fort Starke. They were on the way back, bringing sixty head of horses, when it happened."

For a long moment then Mary was silent. And, watching her closely, Faith waited. "I've never understood exactly what went wrong," Mary said shortly. "We had no warning whatsoever here of any Apaches being off the reservation. It came afterward, when it was too late. But Gentry was caught out on open ground close to a canyon the major had ordered him to avoid. It seems he thought he'd have a better chance of making a stand in the canyon. He turned the horses loose and went in there. He and his sergeant were the only ones to come out alive."

Faith asked softly, "Didn't he ever try and explain?"

"No. At his trial he simply let the facts speak for themselves. He put up no defense at all."

Utter bewilderment was showing in Faith's expression now. "He doesn't seem like the kind of a man who would —"

After a moment Mary said, "Disobey orders? No, he doesn't. Until then he'd been a fine officer. Brilliant, in fact. He had just been given his captaincy well ahead of the time it was expected."

Faith's amazement thinned somewhat, and in this moment Mary saw her as being quite beautiful despite the ugly gash and the swelling high at the hairline along her forehead.

"I had the strangest feeling about him last night," Faith said then. "He seemed so — He's one of those rare people you like and trust immediately."

Something in Mary tightened. She laughed uneasily. "You were very observant, Faith.

Didn't Doctor Spires tell us you were unconscious?"

"That was earlier," Faith told her. "I can remember waking somewhere along the road, can remember his telling me about Mother and Dad. Then later at the doctor's he was so very kind. And — well, so gentle. Just to feel him holding me so close seemed the only thing that kept me from going to pieces."

Mary bridled inwardly at the words, resenting this picture of Gentry having embraced Faith all that long way up the canyon. And she couldn't help saying, "He would be gone for good by now if he hadn't found you. He was on his way out, you know."

If Faith detected any irony in the words she didn't show it; for now she asked, "Then he really is leaving?"

"Yes. They've made it unbearable for him here."

"I was hoping —"

Mary waited a moment. "Hoping what, Faith?"

"Well, that someone could help me with Dad's affairs." Faith laughed uneasily. "Of course it was foolish to hope it might be Captain Gentry."

Mary gave way to an urge then that made her say, "The major has something to tell you, Faith. Something I should perhaps be telling you now. It's about Shotwell."

"Mark Shotwell? Yes, the doctor did say that someone had escaped and brought the word up here. So it was Mark?"

Mary nodded, going on despite a warning voice that told her she was being needlessly unkind. "Major Fitzhugh had him brought up here last night to see what he knew about the — the ownership of that hardware. You see he —"

"But why should they be doubting my word? I kept Dad's books for him!"

"It was because of Caleb Ash, Faith. And Shotwell took Ash's part."

Faith was bewildered and for a long moment couldn't find the words to speak. Then her face took on color and she burst out, "But that's not the truth! I doubt that Mark Shotwell would know. If he does know, he's lying!"

Mary was suddenly feeling ashamed of having broken this news so unfeelingly. Yet now that she had gone this far some contrary impulse drove her even further. "We'll never be able to prove it one way or the other now," she said, putting a false kindliness in her tone. "Shotwell was killed down in town last night. They're hunting the man that did it."

Faith gave such a start that her coffee spilled into the saucer. She reached over and set the cup on the table, a strange calmness settling over her then. "Mark dead? How awful! Murdered, you mean?"

"I'm afraid he was, Faith."

"But why?"

"They don't know yet. Perhaps he'd been drinking and got into a fight. But let's not think about it," Mary added, too lightly.

"I must think about it," Faith said quietly. "No one will believe me now, will they?"

"Isn't there someone back where you came from who could help you?"

"In Denver?" Faith thought a moment. "Perhaps. But what will happen to those wagons meantime?"

"The major didn't say," Mary answered. "You'll have to talk to him about it."

Peebles's detail rode back in across the parade through the drizzle shortly after ten o'clock. When the men had been dismissed, Peebles came straight across to Headquarters, throwing his poncho over saddle after dismounting. On entering Fitzhugh's office he saluted the major precisely and just as precisely gave his report. The wagons were safe in Ash's barn lot, and Ash had promised not to unload any of his goods until he had word from the major that his ownership was no longer questioned.

"And, sir," Peebles said on finishing, "Caleb asked me to give you this." He drew a sealed envelope from his pocket and laid it on the desk.

Fitzhugh's look was puzzled until he had taken the two sheets from the envelope and glanced at them. "An invoice for hardware marked 'Paid.' Signed," he mused on inspecting the first page. He eyed the second then. "And a receipt for eighteen hundred twenty dollars in gold paid to Ash's account, signed by Harry Tipton." He glanced up at his lieutenant. "This is obviously what Caleb was referring to last night as his proof. So the matter's settled."

"So it seems, sir."

Peebles spoke with a faint irony backed with an even fainter smile that made Fitzhugh ask, "You don't think so?"

"Indeed I do." Peebles again reached to the side pocket of his blouse and this time took out a small black book which he laid on the desk in front of the major. "You'll find some very interesting reading there, sir. Very interesting."

Fitzhugh picked up the book.

"What is it?" he asked.

"An account of Tipton's journey across here. Written by his wife. Allow me, sir." Peebles came on around the desk now and reached out to turn several of the pages, continuing, "A chest in their wagon had broken open. It was while we were putting the things back in it that Caleb ran across this. He gave it to me to read."

Fitzhugh glanced up sharply. "You mean you were prying, Mister Peebles?"

The lieutenant's face reddened. "Not at all, sir. Ash looked through it to begin with. He ran onto something extraordinary and showed it to me. It wasn't my intention to pry."

"I understand." Fitzhugh looked down at the book again. "What is it you want to show me?"

"This." Peebles turned another page. "This entry dated the twenty-third of July, just two weeks ago."

He straightened and watched the major read the entry. Then, when Fitzhugh glanced up in puzzlement, he smiled broadly. "Does it mean anything to you, sir?"

"Only what it says." Fitzhugh was frowning. "This Laura Reed had paid Tipton to bring her here."

"Yes, but read on."

Once again the older man scanned the diary. And as he turned to the next page Peebles said, "Now you're coming to it, sir."

After a long moment's silence, Fitzhugh asked, "You're referring to what she says of the striking likeness between her daughter and Laura Reed?"

"Precisely, sir. Same color hair, same eyes, same complexion."

Peebles's smug rejoinder made the major say sharply, "Get to the point, Mister Peebles."

The other at once dropped his faintly patronizing manner. "It occurred to me that the girl found in the wagon yesterday might not really be Tipton's daughter at all, sir."

An expression of outright amazement thawed the severity from Fitzhugh's thin face and, taking encouragement from that, Peebles went on. "On another page Mrs. Tipton discusses the Reed girl at great length. She was very quiet and never talked much about herself. Mrs. Tipton was wondering considerably about her."

Fitzhugh nodded. "Yes. Go on."

"The Reed girl, if she be the one here now," Peebles said quite deliberately, "might very well be making the most of a rare opportunity. Here are these goods without an owner. Or so she assumes. She decides to claim them, pretending to be Tipton's daughter. By the time the matter is straightened out she is gone, leaving no trace of her whereabouts. But for Ash already having paid for his —"

"But you have no proof of what you're saying, Lieutenant!"

Peebles's look took on humility. "No, sir, I haven't. It's only that I thought it best to point out the possibility to you." He drew himself up stiffly, asking, "Was that all, sir?"

Fitzhugh's stern glance thawed somewhat. "Yes. And I suggest we wait a day or so before letting Ash unload those wagons. You may send word down to him that the matter hasn't been decided yet."

The lieutenant saluted and left the room and at once Fitzhugh settled back in his chair and picked up the diary again. Only this time he began with the first page. It took him almost ten minutes to reach the long entry that had so intrigued Peebles. It was the last of all and ran:

Twice today we have observed smoke signals to the north in the direction of the mountains. I shall ask Our Father this night to spare us an encounter with the savages and bring us safely to our journey's end. Laura Reed continues to be an enigma. It is strange to find a girl so young traveling alone. It is even stranger that she should be so self-possessed and worldly. And she seems thoroughly capable of dealing with men. Arthur Williams has been courting her unobtrusively. This morning he asked her to ride with him on a hunt. They were gone for almost an hour, and on their return with a doe I noticed that Arthur's face was red and he seemed disgruntled about something. Laura, however, was her usual self, calm and unruffled. It was obvious that something had passed between them and that Arthur had been rebuffed. This pleases me, for Laura seems to be of good family while Williams is a very common person. I say this not disparagingly, for as a hunter he is excellent, a remarkable shot who has kept us well stocked with fresh game all the way across this wilderness.

Fitzhugh closed the book slowly and sat there tapping his knee with it, frowning in deep thought. Presently he straightened, tossed the diary onto his desk, and, reaching quickly to back pocket for his handkerchief, used it to smother a fit of coughing.

When it was over and his breathing was normal once again he eyed the small book distastefully. Then, seeming to reach a decision, he called, "Sergeant!"

The door opened, and the duty sergeant said ingratiatingly, "Did you call, sir?"

"Yes. Sergeant, will you go to my quarters and ask my daughter to come here? Tell her

I'm sorry to have to ask it but it's unavoidable."

"Very good, sir." The sergeant stepped out, and after the door had closed Fitzhugh sat with elbows on the arms of his swivel chair, hands folded before his pursed lips.

He wondered why it should be that civilian affairs, not military, always vexed him the most and presented the most baffling enigmas. A thought struck him then, *Mary has the grace not to offend,* and his concern lightened somewhat.

Chapter Seven

This had been a long and tiresome morning for Dan Gentry. The cave's gloomy half-light and his weariness had made him sleep far beyond his usual early hour for rising; he hadn't, in fact, wakened until Mike Clears came bringing him a solid breakfast.

The saloonman had refused to discuss last night's happenings, had warned him to stay out of sight, had then hurried away. But there was a gruff friendliness in Clears's manner that was heartening. Gentry was grateful for that.

Gentry spent some time working on the

grulla in the stall next to Clears's big leggy roan horse. He applied ointment to two saddle galls the worn cinch had given the mare in carrying that double load up the canyon yesterday. He forked down hay and filled the mangers for both animals, giving the mare an extra pint of grain. As she ate he curried and brushed her mottled coat. Then he'd repacked his bedroll and tied it to the battered saddle once more.

These chores he had gone about deliberately, wanting to kill time. But his watch said it was still only nine-fifteen when he finished all this and, with nothing but time on his hands, he went to the cave mouth and stood awhile idly looking down on the puddled, rain-swept street.

He saw the wagons crawling slowly up the canyon long before they reached the foot of the street where the road branched to climb the rim. Then, after the column of troopers swung up from the forks, the wagons continuing on along the street, a cool anger stirred in Gentry at realizing the destination of the Conestogas. It surprised him not at all that they climbed as far as Ash's sprawling livery yard and turned in through the gates. *Try and pry 'em loose from him now,* he commented dryly to himself, wondering if anyone was capable of dealing with the situation now even

126

though Faith Tipton should prove her claim to the goods.

As his thoughts shuttled back to the impact of yesterday's stark evidence of the renegades' being on the loose again, he was feeling the Army man's usual scorn for the weak and inept treatment Washington was giving its newest wards. So commonplace had become the breaking of treaties with the Apaches, the use of either weak or openly dishonest agents, the sometimes indiscriminate slaughter of the hostiles when they rebelled, that the best officers in the West had sickened of the spectacle and longed for duty elsewhere. Only the fact of his serving under Robert Fitzhugh, an honest and just man, had kept Gentry from long ago asking for a transfer to some eastern post.

He was making a conscious effort this morning not to think of Faith Tipton and what had happened last night. Yet, try as he would, his mind inevitably turned to her problem, involved enough by Ash's claim and now further complicated by Shotwell's mysterious death. For a time he considered the strangeness of his interest in the girl, wondering at it, puzzled by its having halfway made him forget his own troubles. But then as he looked back on that interval Doc Spires had spent at Headquarters last night he halfway began to understand it. Until those minutes he and the girl had spent alone, Faith Tipton had been simply a woman, might have been any attractive woman, badly in need of help. But by the time Spires returned from his talk with Fitzhugh she had become a person in her own right who attracted him indefinably, powerfully.

Gentry had been on the point of leaving Spires's cabin when the word came that Fitzhugh wanted to see the medico; and Spires had said, "She'd better not be alone, Dan. How about staying with her till I get back?"

Gentry had agreed, and Spires had asked him to sit alongside the bed where the girl lay and hold a hot compress to her gashed forehead. Once the doctor was gone they had begun talking — or rather Faith had talked, shyly at first, and Gentry had listened. Now and then when she fell silent he had prompted her, sensing that this release might be the one thing to give her a grip on her reason and keep her from breaking down completely in the face of the day's tragedy.

At first she had told him of her father and mother, particularly of Harry Tipton's grief two years ago at the loss of his only other child, a son, and of how she had tried to take the boy's place in her father's affections. At that point an odd change had come over her, and now he could recall the husky, low tone of her voice as she abruptly told him, "This is something I mustn't do, Captain, this look-ing back. Dad once told me that the important time for loving someone, for having kindly thoughts of them, is while they're still with you. Now I'm realizing that afterward your thoughts of them are your own and can't be shared with anyone."

That sentiment had held Gentry gravely si-lent before a beginning awareness of a quick and searching intelligence in this girl's make-up, one that was molded by a basically honest and unfettered upbringing. And even now that facet of her nature intrigued him far more than her delicate beauty.

She had talked of other things then, asking about his life on the post and about the town. Her father had hoped to settle here in Elk Bend and start in business. Rather than disturb her by any mention of his own trou-bles, Gentry hadn't once talked about him-self. She had heard Spires calling him Captain. She had called him that and he hadn't corrected her.

Now, trying to analyze his unsettling feelings toward the girl, he knew only that he deeply respected her, that more than her physical at-tractiveness lay behind the quickened interest so unlike any he had ever before experienced toward a woman. And he had a queer feeling that he was betraying something in his own make-up in leaving here before she had found someone who could look after her affairs.

Rarely had he experienced such a complete sense of helplessness as now. In a way this circumstance was akin to that of the day on which he had lost his detail in the wild canyon far to the south. Then, as now, he had been powerless to change anything, to ward off the inevitable.

This was his frame of mind when, shortly after eleven o'clock, he saw Mike Clears come plodding down the puddled mire of the alley, cross the creek by the narrow bridge, and start up this way along the wheel ruts, his stocky frame cloaked in a shapeless poncho. The drizzle was laying a constant rustling whisper across the stillness, and the dampness sharpened the sweet aroma of the hay and the faint ammoniac tang of the stables issuing from the cave.

Clears lost his footing once in his climb and barely sprawled in the mud, and Gentry plainly caught the man's ripe oath. It made him smile, and that humor was still showing on his lean face when Clears shortly strode up to him.

Gentry's amusement was short-lived, however. For Mike Clears's blocky features were set in stubborn anger as he roughly stomped the mud from his boots and flung the poncho to the dirt just inside the cave mouth.

The saloonman's first words were an explosive "Damn 'em! Damn 'em all!"

"Who, Mike?"

For his answer, Clears held out a folded piece of paper. Gentry took it, opened it, and read:

Sir:

Knowing that you had made a business arrangement with Mr. Harry Tipton and undoubtedly owe him freight on goods he was transporting here when he suffered his misfortune, I feel it my duty to advise you of certain facts. There is now some question as to the identity of the woman found alive yesterday in Tipton's wagon. Two women answering the general description of the survivor were aboard the wagons, one being Tipton's daughter, the other a young woman known as Laura Reed. In view of the strong possibility that the female found alive may be Laura Reed, and not Miss Tipton, I caution you against making any settlement with her on monies owed Harry Tipton for his services. Should you care to discuss this matter further with me I shall be at your disposal. Meantime, I remain,

Y'rs obediently,
Signed: Robert L. Fitzhugh
Major, Cavalry, U.S. Army

Gentry's glance whipped up to the saloon-man, his eyes ablaze with indignation. But before he could speak Clears was saying hurriedly, "Wait'll you hear the rest! I'm just back from a talk with Fitzhugh. He showed me a journal Tipton's wife had kept on their way here. The woman had some questions in her mind about this Reed girl, and Fitzhugh's making his guesses from that."

"But can't the Old Man see this girl's honest and decent as he is?" Gentry's voice was unsteady with anger.

"It's not a question of decency," Clears told him. "Honesty perhaps, but the Reed girl was apparently decent enough. It's that Laura Reed was — well, an adventuress, maybe. Hell, all I know is that Ash has raised this stink by turning up with a receipt for payment of his goods! Fitzhugh says you can't argue against that."

"If Faith Tipton's arguing it, then so am I!"

Clears's glance sharpened. But all he said was, "Here, too."

Gentry turned, doubled his fist, and hit the dirt wall behind him a solid, savage blow. Then, turning back again, he asked helplessly, "What's going to happen to her, Mike?"

"It's already happened. They've moved her out of the major's cabin into one of the huts

132

alongside the washer women. Fitzhugh's daughter took care of that, damn her! Gave her some cock-and-bull story about their needing the room she was in for a visiting officer. She hadn't heard a word about this question of who she is till I went to call on her. I lost my head and showed her Fitzhugh's note. It knocked her flat. The only thing in her favor's that Fitzhugh isn't letting Ash unload those wagons till everything's settled."

Gentry's lean face had lost color, and his voice had a grating edge to it now as he asked, "Anything else?"

"Yeah. About Shotwell. Fitzhugh had him up there last night asking him about Ash's claim on having paid for his goods. He must've been killed right after he got back down here. Said he knew it for a fact."

"He didn't!" Gentry breathed barely audibly. And when Mike Clears only nodded, he drawled, "There goes my hunch. I'd have bet money it was Ash that cut Shotwell down."

"So I'd thought. But as it turns out, Caleb had every reason to want Shotwell to stay alive. To back his own claim."

There was a long moment's silence between them that ended as Gentry said, "This morning you told me Tipton had been up here several months ago, Mike. If Shotwell was with him that trip, couldn't he have worked up a grudge with someone here back then? Whoever had it in for him must've got to him last night when he got back down here from the post."

"That could be. I'll have Ralph Blake check on it."

Gentry was eyeing the saloonman closely and now abruptly asked, "Do you belive it, Mike? After seeing that girl and talking to her? Do you believe any part of it?"

"Hell, no!"

Mike Clears surprised himself by the readiness of his answer. He had been so pressed for time this morning, so confounded by these unexpected developments, that he hadn't had time to ask himself the questions Gentry had just put. Now, sure that his answer would have been the same had he deliberated upon it at length, he felt a strange and indefinable relief, adding, "In case you think I'm talking through the hat, friend, come back and help me hitch up the buggy. I'm going back up there."

"What for?"

"To get Faith Tipton and bring her down here. I'm putting her in my room above the office. I can hole up here in the cave as long as she wants to use my place. She'll probably be taking the stage out as soon as it's running again. My hangout's not much, but there's no other fit place for a girl like her in this town."

Gentry was momentarily struck by the incongruity of the statement, by Clears' assuming that a room over the back of a saloon was what he claimed it to be, a fit place for a decent woman to stay. But then Gentry knew that the room above the *Lucky Find*'s office was exactly that; it was isolated from the rest of the building and Clears, regardless of his profession, was a gentleman in every sense of the word. Furthermore, as he had said, there wasn't so much as a boardinghouse in this mushrooming, raw camp where a woman would want to stay.

The saloonman misread Gentry's preoccupation now and stated dryly, "I'll even give her a key so she can lock herself in."

"Wasn't thinking of that, Mike." The sober set of Gentry's lean face didn't change an iota as he added, "You spoke of bedding down up here. Do you snore?"

Clears frowned. "Don't know. But what if I do?"

"It'll bother me. I'm a light sleeper."

"But you were headed out —" A dawning look of understanding thinned Clears's puzzlement, to be replaced immediately by a worried look. "You mean you're staying on?"

"Right."

Clears swallowed with difficulty before he said haltingly, "Aren't you forgetting, Dan? You might run into trouble with the first man that lays eyes on you. Not everybody's looking at this the way I —"

"Save your wind, Mike," Gentry interrupted mildly. "I'm staying. There were a couple of things I wanted to find out anyway. Now I can look around and maybe help the girl at the same time."

Over a moment's deliberate silence Clears spoke one word. "Ash?"

"He's tied in with it," Gentry admitted. Then he drawled pointedly, "I don't have a thing to lose in this, Mike. You do. You're sure you want to help the girl and buy into this with me?"

"Good God, how strong do I have to make it?" Clears flared.

Those words laid a smile across Gentry's face. "Then while you're up above after Faith, hunt up Tim McCune and tell him something for me."

"Tell him what?"

It took Gentry a good quarter-minute to answer that. At first Clears was puzzled. He interrupted twice with questions. Then shortly they were arguing, Gentry speaking quietly, Clears's face finally going slack in amazement at something Gentry had said.

Some minutes later they turned in from the cave mouth and strode on back past the stalls toward the buggy. It was then that the saloonman said dryly, awkwardly, nevertheless meaning it, "I've been thinking some pretty ornery things about you, Dan. Can I take 'em back?"

Gentry looked around with a grin. "My hide's thick, friend."

"I know. But I've been wrong to believe everything they said about you."

"Nothing's changed. I'm the same man I was yesterday."

"But I'm not. I'll eat my crow and like it."

Mike Clears's buggy left the post shortly after noon, and Mary Fitzhugh, happening to be looking out across the rain-fogged parade, saw it as it pulled out from the end hutment along Laundry Row. At the last possible moment she recognized Faith Tipton sitting beside the driver, who was someone she didn't know.

The afternoon was half gone before Mary's curiosity got the best of her and she contrived to meet Tim McCune on his way to the stables. As a result of their meeting the sergeant generously offered to drive her down to town on some errands. He'd been headed down there anyway, he said. And on their way along the bench road in the major's buggy, Mary expertly guided the conversation. McCune at first hedged in giving any definite answers to her seemingly innocent questions. But then, succumbing to her charm and a casual reminder of how she had managed to deliver the clothes to Gentry yesterday morning, he told her of his reason for visiting town. Gentry had sent for him. The result was that her errands were forgotten and he took her to the *Lucky Find*'s rear entrance.

Swinging down out of the buggy before the tie rail there, he told her, "You won't want to come in. I'll bring Mike out here."

"What kind of a man is he, Sergeant?"

"You'll like him."

While Mary sat there alone in the buggy, her hands under the buffalo robe because of the damp chill, she was trembling with anticipation. She had supposed that Dan Gentry was by now well out through the foothills on his way to Santa Fe. She was delighted at the prospect of seeing him once more. She hoped this saloon owner wouldn't be difficult and refuse to take her to Gentry. She would treat the man aloofly and in her customary manner when dealing with tradesmen.

Presently, she heard the door open and looked up across the platform. It was Dan Gentry and not a stranger who stood there looking down at her. And in her surprise and delight she smiled radiantly, not caring that he should see how pleased she was.

He was hatless, wearing the same outfit she

had yesterday given him, the jutting of the holstered gun at his thigh somehow accenting his erect carriage. Though his sober look was slightly disconcerting it was what she had almost come to expect of him.

She laughed now as she saw the rain pelting his head and shoulders, calling, "Dan, you'll be soaked! Come sit here." And she lifted the buffalo robe from her lap, holding a corner of it over the far side of the seat.

He came on down the steps then, and she noticed as she had countless other times how effortlessly his big frame seemed to move. The buggy lurched against his weight, and as she laid the robe across his knees she said, "I hadn't expected this. You should have sent me word you were staying."

"Didn't know it myself till a few hours ago." He was regarding her now with no break whatsoever in his gravity. Bluntly then, unexpectedly, he asked, "How could you turn her out like that, Mary?"

She stiffened, knowing now what lay behind his seriousness. "Turn her out? Why shouldn't I? The major wanted it. So did I."

"You should have told her why you were doing it."

"Should I be called upon to make explanations to a person like that?" she asked indignantly.

139

He smiled, very faintly. "You and the Old Man both believe she's this Reed girl?"

"I certainly do."

"And he hasn't made up his mind about her?" When she didn't reply, he drawled, "I thought so."

Anger brightened the look in her eyes. "It's there for everyone to see, Dan! First her lying about the hardware, then the things Mrs. Tipton wrote about her. Have you — aren't you letting the fact that you carried her up here in your arms, that she may be pretty in a calculating way, warp your judgment?"

His face took on color. "What are you trying to say, Mary?"

"I believe Mrs. Tipton said it in her diary. Laura Reed has a way with men."

His eyes were blazing with a strong indignation, and, seeing that, she tried to look contrite as she slipped her hand through the bend of his arm, murmuring, "Dan, we mustn't let a thing like this come between us! I only — only hope you won't let her make a fool of you. Sergeant McCune says you're trying to help her, you and this Clears person."

"We are." His tone was clipped, hard.

"How, Dan?" she asked meekly.

His glance swung away from her and he said tonelessly, "One way would be to keep Ash

140

from selling those goods till she proves they're hers."

"But isn't he holding the wagons in his yard?"

"Just now he is."

She sensed some obscure meaning behind his words and said urgently, "You must be careful of that man! I heard about your fighting him last night. You can't hope to be that lucky again."

He reached down to take her hand and lift his arm away; and as he moved to the seat's edge she realized she had once again said the wrong thing. "I didn't mean that the way it sounded, Dan! It's just that you're running such risks in staying here." She clung tightly to his hand. "This woman isn't worth it! Aren't things bad enough for you as they are?"

"A man does what he sees he has to."

"But she's only taking advantage of you!"

"We'll see," he drawled, stepping aground. He glanced at her briefly to say, "McCune will take you back home," before he turned up the steps. He didn't pause or look back on his way in across the platform to Mike Clears's office door.

He found Tim McCune alone in there, and his voice was gruff as he said, "She's ready to go back now. And not a word to her about tonight."

141

McCune's look was uncomfortable. "Guess I told her too much, Captain."

"No, it's not that. We're just being careful."

The sergeant went to the alley door. "You said eight, Captain?"

Gentry nodded. "Eight." But then, as McCune was reaching for the door, he said, "Wait a minute, Tim." After a slight pause, he asked, "Did you hear about last night?"

"About Shotwell?"

"No, about my tangling with Ash up there at the gate."

"No!"

Gentry gave a slow tilt of the head. "We had a scrap. Johnny Ewing wound it up by clubbing me with his rifle."

McCune's look was instantly outraged; and at that Gentry asked, "Why would Ewing side with Caleb? He tried to kill me."

The sergeant burst out, "I've been itchin' to whittle that lad down to size! Now I'll —"

"But what I'm after is why he'd jump me when Ash called for him to do it," Gentry interrupted. "Why would he?"

McCune lifted hands outward in an unknowing gesture. "Search me." Abruptly he frowned. "Unless —"

When he didn't go on, Gentry asked, "Unless what?"

After a moment's hesitation, the sergeant

said, "You know about the game Ash runs in his barn every payday, how slick he is with the cards? Well, a couple weeks ago I heard he was into some of the boys for some real money. Ewing owed him close to two hundred. Which is probably why Johnny's turned up sober the last few times he was paid. But then last week he got paid and hit the booze again. It got me to wondering. How could he if he owes Ash?"

Gentry's look was a deeply thoughtful one. And shortly he mused aloud, "It could be. Ewing could have passed the word to him."

McCune stiffened, instantly catching his meaning. "So he could!" he breathed. "He knew about our going to Starke, knew about bringing the remounts back. He told Ash, and Ash got the word to the 'Paches!"

"Maybe, Tim. Just maybe." Gentry sighed, saying then, "Keep an eye on Ewing. You may run across something."

"I've had my eye on him, sir."

Gentry nodded. "Good. Now you'd better get out there to Mrs. Fitzhugh."

McCune started to salute, but Gentry's shake of the head cut him short, and he went out. And afterward Gentry took the chair at the desk, contemplating something that etched a deep gravity across his face.

Chapter Eight

The sun broke through just before it set, reflecting from the cloud mass lifting off Sentinel a last burst of brilliant orange light that sharpened the colors along the canyon — the light emerald of the aspen, the darker shade of pine, the yellow-brown undulations of the placers. The air was sharp, chill, laden with a heady freshness that bore strongly the pleasing taint of new-washed earth.

Caleb Ash worked through the dusk and then on into the evening by lantern light, nailing down tar paper he had this morning hastily spread over the unshingled sheathing on the roof of his hardware store to protect it from the rain. Ned Stroble was the last stable hand to leave and as he was closing the big gates he called up, "Any word on when we start unloadin' those wagons, Boss?"

"None." Ash swore soundly. "But we do it tomorrow regardless."

Stroble said, "Good. To hell with those Army stuffed shirts." And he turned and walked off down the muddy street.

At about this time Tim McCune, bellied up

to the bar in the *Lucky Find,* saw the man he had been waiting for come in through the swing-doors. He was in luck, for Trooper Andrews spotted him standing there and pushed his way through the crowd. As he came in alongside, Andrews said pleasantly, "Man needs something to thaw out his gizzard on a night like this, eh, Sergeant? Thought this was summer."

"Think again," McCune said. Then, as Andrews was nodding to an apron, asking for a bottle, McCune asked, "Did you find him?"

Andrews looked around.

"Find who?"

"Ash. Caleb Ash. I hear you were looking for him."

"Not me."

McCune scowled. "You mean to say you weren't just in here asking where you could locate Ash?" When Andrews had shaken his head, McCune muttered, "Guess this gent that told me about it mistook some other bird for you."

He eyed the trooper obliquely a moment, then abruptly said, "Look, Andrews. Do me a favor. Whoever was looking for Ash said it was important. The major wants to see him right away. If you'll go up there to the yard and make sure he got the word, your drink's on me when you get back. And don't mention me, or Ash won't pay any attention. We don't get on too well."

"He and me either," Andrews said, turning from the counter. "Be back in five minutes." And he headed for the street.

McCune turned slowly then and glanced back toward Mike Clears's office. Gentry was leaning there in the shadows by the door, and now McCune tilted his head in a slow, unmistakable nod. He waited until he saw Gentry disappear into the office. Then, picking up his drink, he sighed gustily. His hand was shaking.

Ash was still on the roof of his new building when Andrews walked up out of the darkness and called to him. The scout listened to the trooper's story. Someone, Andrews didn't know who, was looking for him to take him up to see Fitzhugh. It was urgent. No, Andrews didn't know what it was all about; he'd heard of it second or maybe third hand.

Caleb Ash, astride his bay gelding, left the yard even before Andrews had had time to get back to the *Lucky Find* and collect his drink. And Ash hadn't been gone quite one minute when Dan Gentry crossed the street from the shadows of a wide vacant stretch on the far side, opened the gate, and disappeared into the yard.

Over quite an interval then subdued sounds

issued from the stable lot, noises that several passers-by scarcely noticed because they were the usual to be heard from a stable — the stomp of horses, the rattle of doubletree chains, the creak of axles.

Finally Gentry appeared at the gate once more. He looked both ways along the street before he pushed the gate's two halves wide open. He went back out of sight then toward a high gray shape that showed against the yard's blackness and shortly his voice sounded in an urgently-spoken word, followed by the report of a whiplash.

Seconds later three teams lunging powerfully against harness pulled a canvas-shrouded Conestoga out into the street and straight across it. Close behind the first lumbering wagon came another, its tongue chained to the back axle of the first; then finally, blocking the whole width of the street, a third followed the second.

Gentry stood erect and with legs braced against the seat of the first Conestoga as he reined the teams off into the blackness across the street toward the creek. Down there some twenty minutes ago he had marked a fairly good crossing by the irregular shape of a boulder. And now as that shape came up out of the dark brushy void stretching ahead of his lead team he swung the animals sharply left, using the whip again even though this was a downgrade and the wagons were rolling faster.

The high-bodied Conestoga lurched violently as its wheels dropped into the creek, jolted over the rocky bottom, then lifted over the far bank. Seconds later Gentry used the whip mercilessly as he felt the wagon abruptly slow again, nearly stop. Almost immediately and for several seconds the horses moved the load faster as the second wagon lurched across the stream. Then there was another interval when it seemed the animals were pulling at the side of a mountain. The wagons slowed, came to a standstill.

Gradually the load started inching forward again, and now Gentry booted the brake-arm as far forward as it would go and held his weight against it. For this was a steep downgrade and the ground was rough, strewn with small boulders. Once the wagon's tongue slewed dangerously around to bring the off-wheel horse to his knees. It was mainly Gentry's brute, rawhide strength on the reins that hauled the animal to its feet again.

Presently, off across the creek, the lights of the store windows let him make out the silhouettes of buildings and he took his boot from the brake, letting the horses go on at a faster trot. Somewhere close ahead were the pair of wheel ruts that crossed the stream and began climbing toward the cave mouth. He began using the whip again.

The lead Conestoga lumbered suddenly into the wheel ruts. Gentry pulled the leaders sharp right along the road and as the teams lunged into the upgrade they slowed from a trot to a slow walk. Two figures standing beside the narrow roadway slid past in the darkness and then, when the wagons were barely moving, Gentry called, "That'll do it!" and stood on the brake again.

Mike Clears and Tim McCune, both breathing heavily at the weight they carried, stepped in on the second and third wagons at Gentry's cry. Clears dropped a sixty-pound pine log squarely behind the rear wheels of the second wagon and sighed relievedly as the wheel rims rocked back against it, solidly wedged. Tim McCune had more trouble blocking the last wagon; it was only when it had jolted to a stop against its chain and slewed around two feet out of the ruts that he managed to get his log under both wheels.

They worked fast then, speaking only a word or two. Once Clears called softly, "More slack!" and Gentry eased up on the brake to let the first wagon roll back another foot. Shortly afterward the saloonman's voice sounded out of the shadows back there again.

"Let 'er roll!" and Gentry slapped his teams with the reins, using the whip once more.

The first Conestoga rolled slowly up through the darkness and finally in on the narrow shelf before the cave mouth. Gentry turned his teams into the cave and heard the canvas scrape the top of the rocky arch, heard a hickory bow snap. He drove straight on toward the feeble light of a lantern far back in the cavern, and as the horses plodded into the light Mike Clears and Tim McCune ran up alongside the wagon's front wheels, Clears shortly calling, "This'll do."

They unhitched the teams and quickly took them on down the slope again. The second wagon seemed heavier than the first and on its way up Clears and McCune took hold of the wheel spokes and threw their strength into moving it against the hard climb.

It was when they were unhitching the teams from the second wagon that Gentry said impatiently, "We're taking too much time! Ash knows something's wrong by now. You bring up that last one. Mike, where's the crowbar?"

"Lyin' right outside. Can you do it alone?"

Gentry nodded and started out from the light toward the cave mouth. He had gone only several strides when he halted abruptly, asking, "What about your horses?"

"The roan's tied down there where you wanted him. I'm leaving the mare here."

"Is there whisky enough down there to last you?"

"No, damn it! If there was it'd look like I had a hand in this. It's supposed to be a plain act of God, remember?"

"So it is," Gentry drawled. "Give me a whistle when everything's clear down here." And he walked on out.

He found the crowbar lying along the wall just outside the cave mouth and as he hefted it he stood a moment working at the buckle of his shell belt, thinking that the Colt's riding his thigh would be in the way for what was to come. But then he knew that if he left the weapon anywhere but in the cave he would lose it and, since everything depended on how fast he moved from now on, he finally hurried on still wearing it.

For the first fifty yards his climb up the slope above the cave was comparatively easy. But then he reached the steeper going where the face of the rim was almost sheer and he had to pick his way slowly, often using as much of the strength of his arms as his legs in pulling himself up across the ledges. The crowbar slipped from his grasp once, and he slid downward ten feet after letting go a handhold to catch it.

Shortly he caught Mike Clears's low whistle from below, which would mean that the last wagon was in the cave and that Clears and Tim McCune were on their way down to the creek to turn Ash's teams out.

Finally, an endless ten minutes after the saloonman's signal, Gentry lay belly-down on a broad ledge that hung directly over the opening to the cave, a good hundred feet above it. He was gasping for breath, his chest aching as he dragged in deep lungfuls of air. But even so he got to his knees and crawled on over to the far side of the ledge, worried by the knowledge that the moving of the wagons and getting up here had taken far too long. Caleb Ash was certainly back in town by now.

Beyond the ledge's far corner was a two-foot-wide shelf that jutted from the face of the cliff. Gentry had studied it from below at the window of Mike Clears's office late this afternoon when he had first seen the possibility of hiding Faith Tipton's wagons. And now as he stood on this shelf and thrust the crowbar's tapered end into a crevice below the ledge's top strata of crumbling sandstone, he was thinking of Faith, wondering if this gamble would give her the time she so sorely needed to prove how wrong Ash's claim was.

He threw his weight against the crowbar

and felt the heavy slab of rock lifting. Just then he heard a sifting of loose pebbles go rattling down the slope below. He paused, straightening, listening to the sound. Finally he placed it as coming from well below and in the up-canyon direction he had taken in making his climb. He decided it must be either the falling of rock he had loosened in his climb or it was Mike Clears coming up here to help him.

He hunched over and levered the limestone slab upward once more, smiling at the thought of how surprised Mike Clears would shortly be if he was on his way up here. Then suddenly the night's stillness was shattered by a shotgun's blasting roar coming at him from out of the blackness below.

Mike Clears, waiting at the open alley window of his darkened office, went rigid as the reverberating blasts of two gunshots ripped away the heavy mantle of the night's stillness. For perhaps five seconds as the racketing echoes ran back and forth along the canyon's corridor he stood there gripped by strong alarm, a sudden fear for Dan Gentry.

Then came an earth-jarring pound from high along the rim face. It was so solid that he could faintly feel the floor quiver. And immediately afterward there was a low rumble gaining in volume until shortly the air vibrated with a sound not unlike that of a big ore wagon crossing a heavy-planked bridge.

Now the whole building shook with the gathering roar. The two office doors rattled, and the metal shade on the desk lamp clanged against its braces. He could plainly hear the sharp explosive racketing of heavy boulders striking the rim's lower ledges. Then he caught the heavy undertone of a massive slide.

Though he had been waiting for this, expecting it at any moment, the unlooked-for magnitude of what was happening awed Mike Clears to a degree that left him shaken, almost disbelieving. Only when a gray fog of rock dust billowed in through the window did he stir from his paralysis of utter amazement and reach out to pull down the sash. Then, as the night out there swallowed the last dying sounds and finally turned utterly still, he remembered the gunshots once more and was again afraid, really afraid.

He was trying to understand the shots, telling himself that some drunk on a spree must have fired them, when the first shouts echoed in off the street. Then abruptly Faith Tipton's light step crossed the room above and the door at the head of the narrow stairway opened to let a shaft of lamplight pattern the upper part of the office's far wall.

Though he couldn't see the stairhead he

knew Faith must be standing there holding the lamp, listening. She was probably afraid, wanting not to be alone. She was also doubtless wanting some explanation of the terrifying sounds she heard. But Mike Clears stood as he was, not wishing to have to explain to her just yet. He and Gentry had purposely been vague in telling her of their plans tonight. And just now, filled with apprehension for Gentry's safety, he decided that she should know nothing of what had happened until he was sure himself of exactly what it was.

After several seconds the door up there closed, and quite plainly Clears heard her step cross the room once more. That sound irritated him. For, having gone to some pains giving Faith absolute privacy, he was reminded now that she would have little of it until he put a board over the six-inch circular flue opening in the outside corner of the office's ceiling. Two months ago he had taken the stove out of the office, taken down the stovepipe that climbed up through the corner of his bedroom to give the only heat he ever needed up there. He had meant to cover the hole this afternoon when he and Gentry were in the room talking with Faith; but it had slipped his mind. Now he could plainly hear any sound from the room above and realized that any from down here would undoubtedly disturb Faith.

His preoccupation over this irritating over-sight was abruptly ended by an excited mutter of voices in the alley. Because he knew that Faith might hear him moving around, and because he didn't want her to know that he had been standing here all this time, he walked soundlessly across to the saloon door, opened it, slammed it, and then came back across the office to his desk with a heavy tread. He lit the lamp there and immediately went on out into the alley.

Someone in the crowd there spotted him and came up to take a tight hold on his arm, saying, "Look, Mike! God-amighty, look!"

The saloonman was looking. Several men with lanterns were standing down by the creek, two of them beyond it, and what the pale glow of the lanterns showed him made Clears swear softly in awe. A mass of boulders and rubble half choked the stream. Beyond, a torn heap of rubble slanted up sharply. Mike Clears's imagining of what this was to look like hadn't prepared him in any degree for the reality of it. There had been a narrow stretch of level ground across there footing the road climbing to the cave. Now a steep mass of rock rubble slanted down from the rim face all the way to the creek. There was no trace of road, of bench, or cave mouth. A huge section of the lower rim had settled into the canyon bottom.

"Wasn't your whisky kept up there, Mike?" asked the man alongside now. "What do we do for drinks?"

"You drink up what's inside here and then go dry." As Clears spoke he remembered the part he had to play and asked, "Anyone know how it happened?"

"No. But one of the boys says he heard a shotgun up there right before she cut loose."

"A shotgun? Doesn't make sense."

"None of it does," came the man's answer.

Clears turned back up the steps to his office, suddenly worried with this added proof of something he hadn't dared quite believe. There really had been a shotgun up there; his hearing hadn't played tricks on him after all. And now the mystery of that gun was added to his misgivings over Gentry having survived the falling in of the rim.

Mike Clears went on through the office and into the near-empty saloon, at once calling for whisky. He downed one glass quickly, then another. And the apron who served him, observing this rarity, observed solemnly, "A close call, eh, Boss?"

"Too close, Fred."

Clears was standing with his back to the street, scarcely noticing the banging of the doors as the crowd began filling the place

157

again. His thoughts were somber, indrawn. Suddenly they were rudely jarred by a voice close behind him saying, "I'll have a word with you, Mike."

Clears knew that voice. He turned with a studied slowness that nicely hid his surprise. He had to tilt his head to meet Caleb Ash's cold glance. It made him say casually, "Sure, Caleb. Where'll it be, here or in the office?"

"Back there."

Ash's words grated with suppressed fury and, with this added warning of something quite unexpected in prospect, Clears led the way on back along the bar. When he reached his office door he let Ash enter the room first.

He had barely closed the door when Ash was saying, "I saw him up there! Looked at him right over the barrels of my Greener. I think I got him."

A sickening feeling of acute dread settled through Clears. And along with the unmistakable meaning behind Ash's words came the sudden realization that Faith Tipton must be hearing them. His glance quickly lifted to the flue hole. Yet he was utterly poker-faced an instant later as he looked around at the scout to drawl, "You'll have to speak plainer, Caleb. Should I know what you're talking about?"

"You damn well should!" Ash blazed. "They say you've taken that girl in. You and

Gentry did it for her!"

"Did what?" Clears asked the question only to cover his move to the desk. He eased down into the chair behind it.

"Tolled me up to the fort on that snipe hunt! Hauled my wagons out of the yard and up to your cave! All that rock didn't bust loose on its own!"

Mike Clears sighed softly, knowing now that there was no possible way to keep Faith from hearing the whole story. "You're right about the rock, Caleb. Those weak ledges were bound to fall some day. Should have blasted 'em down myself long ago. But what's this other?"

Ash's coarse face darkened in fury at the blandness of the question. "All right, damn you, play it dumb! But from now on watch yourself! Beginnin' now, tonight, I'm hirin' a crew to muck out that rock and get those wagons back. Just don't get in my way!"

Mike Clears shook his head in a baffled way. Then, feeling of his vest pockets as though in search of a cigar, he looked down and lazily reached over to pull open the top drawer of his desk. He let his hand rest on the drawer's edge.

His glance had been meek until now. But as it lifted to meet Ash's once more his expression was startlingly cold and hard.

"Caleb," he said tonelessly, "here's some free advice. Never accuse a man of anything you can't prove against him. Even if you can prove it, never toss it at him unless you're set to back your play!"

His fingers lifted from the drawer's edge. "There's a gun here. You're wearing one. Either go for yours or get out! Now!"

Ash's massive frame drew straighter under the sting of those words. He stood stock-still, his eyes coming wider open. They shuttled down to the drawer, then back to Clears's face. His right hand clawed slightly. For a long moment it looked as though that hand would slash up to the holster higher along his thigh.

But all at once his fingers relaxed. "We'll save it for another day," he said. "Anyway, I know now where you stand in this."

"Get out, Caleb!"

The scout slowly turned to the door, arrogantly taking his time. Before he opened it he glanced back to say, "We'll keep an eye out for your friend while we dig that rock away."

Clears said nothing, though the words cut him sharply. He watched Ash throw the door wide and step on out, leaving it open. He had leaned forward in the chair, about to get up and go across there, when a slighter, smaller figure came through the door.

160

Ben Qualls was the last person Mike Clears expected to see just now. The swamper evidently noticed his nervous manner, for as he came on in he said dryly, "Got you jumpy, too, has it? I was half a mile above when she cut loose. Must've sounded like the whole mountain comin' in on you down here."

"It did, Ben." Clears slumped down in the chair again. Then, remembering, he added, "You're back too soon. I told you to get everything you could."

"Which is what I did. Could've been back sooner. But I waited to make sure of what they're sayin' about *Gonah-Dokoh*."

Mike Clears was again remembering the chimney hole. But now he reasoned that Faith, having heard what Ash had said of Gentry, might just as well know what Ben Qualls was to say about him; this might even help ease the shock of the news Ash had brought.

So he asked, "What are they saying?"

"That Sour Eye's dead. That a column from Fort Starke wiped out his band 'way south of here. They been smoke-talkin' about it all afternoon."

Clears's worried expression eased a trifle. "Well, at least that's a help. Do you believe it?"

Ben Qualls shrugged his bony shoulders. "They usually know things before we do.

Sure I believe it."

"What about the other, Ben? What I sent you down there for?"

The old swamper gave a spare smile, shaking his head in a wondering way. "Mike, you won't believe it. Get yourself set for a jolt," he began. And then he told the rest.

The slam of the office door below seemed to snap the tension holding Faith; and, a sudden weakness engulfing her, she reached out and steadied herself against the window's sill. She had heard every word that passed between Qualls and Clears. Earlier, trying at first not to listen, then having to listen, she had heard enough of Ash's booming talk to grasp the enormity of the news he was bringing Clears. Earlier still, lying in bed and nearly asleep, the rumbling roar of the rockslide had left her terrified and feeling very alone.

And now the dread certainty that Dan Gentry had died tonight, died while trying to help her, was insistently threatening to beat aside her stubborn hope that he had somehow survived. An overwhelming grief and fear engulfed her, and she buried her face in her fisted hands, fighting to strengthen the conviction that in the beginning Ash hadn't seemed too sure of himself. She was frantically groping for remembrance of something he had said shortly after entering the office, something she had lain there trying not to overhear.

In this moment there came the stark realization of how much Dan Gentry meant to her. Unaccountably, yet surely, he had somehow managed to buoy up her spirits today and make her look beyond the tragedy of yesterday and into the future with a new sense of wanting to face it. His calm, sure way of accepting his own misfortune had shown her how to face hers. Never in such a short space of time — in any length of time, for that matter — had she come to admire and respect a man so unreservedly as she did this one.

And now Dan Gentry was gone!

She had reached that low point in her jumbled thinking when the rebellion in her won out over the doubt. And now an abrupt impulse turned her from the window to the bed. She began hurriedly dressing, thinking back upon the afternoon, upon as much as Gentry and Clears had told her of their plans. They had been purposely vague, probably because they didn't want her to worry. But one thing she did remember. Clears had said he was bringing a horse down to a shed along the alley after dark — "the last one down on the creek side," was how he had put it. The animal would be saddled and carrying a bedroll and rifle.

Gentry was leaving, leaving for good; or so she had concluded. All the late afternoon and evening that fact had depressed her. She had supposed she would never see him again. Perhaps she never would, but she must know one way or the other if he still lived.

This morning when he had come to get her at the fort, Clears had given her his rough wool overcoat to wear. She pulled that on over her dress now, softly opened the door at the head of the stairway and looked down into the office. The lamp was on down there, but the room was quiet, certainly empty. As she started quickly down the stairway she dismissed any thought of sharing with Clears her slender hope that Gentry still lived; he would think it nothing but a womanly intuition, would probably forbid her going out into the night.

She stopped there on the steps as soon as she could look down into the room, wanting to make sure she was alone. A lazy ribbon of smoke from a cigar curled up across the desk lamp's cone of light. The air was stale, smelling strongly of the cigar, and for a moment Faith experienced an overpowering feeling of physical and mental confinement. As she hurried down the stairway and then out the alley door, she had a sense of each step bringing her closer to a welcome release, closer to Dan Gentry.

Hesitating outside at the foot of the platform, she drew the coat more tightly about her, then turned down the alley. The air had a chill bite to it, and before she had gone ten steps through the alley's mire she was feeling the dampness through her shoes and an icy grip about her ankles. But she was glad to be out here and alone with her thoughts. Had it not been for that disheartening doubt as to what the next few minutes were to bring, she would have been almost happy.

She was abreast a building some distance below the saloon when suddenly the opening of a door close by brought her to a startled stop. A rectangle of light abruptly lay across the alley directly ahead, and the sound of voices and the tinny beat of a piano coming from the building intruded upon the night's peaceful stillness. A man wearing a flour-sacking apron stepped out the door to empty a bucket into the impenetrable shadows. He stood there scanning the darkness, for a moment looking squarely at Faith. But then he turned and stepped back out of sight, and the door closed. And Faith hurried on, her momentary uneasiness quickly leaving her.

Now that her eyes were accustomed to the darkness, she could make out the vague shapes of buildings. Those to her left, streetward, presently became more widely spaced and

165

then gave way to tents and a scattering of slab shacks. On the side of the creek she passed a barn, two smaller sheds. Beyond them she stopped, thinking that the last shed she had passed must be the one Clears had meant.

Then, far ahead, she made out the indistinct shape of another small building. She walked on to it. Approaching it, she experienced a heady anticipation as she plainly heard the muffled stomp of a horse inside. She hurried on to the shed and found the door on the far side. The hinges squealed loudly as she opened the door.

The pitch-blackness of the shed's interior was so complete that it gave her a sense of walking into nothingness. She took two halting steps and stopped, wishing now that she had thought to bring along some sulphur matches. Suddenly she heard the horse's moving close by; she spoke gently and then stretched out a hand and moved in the direction of the animal. Her hand abruptly touched him, and he moved quickly away, and she spoke again, feeling of his shoulder, then his neck.

When the animal had quieted, she worked her hand slowly back from his neck until it touched the smooth and rounded swell of a saddle. Her heart quickened its beat as her hand groped to the saddle's far side, her fingers brushing the stock of a rifle. She reached back and felt the shape of a bedroll and knew that this must be the roan.

But then her strong excitement over having found the animal at once subsided before a feeling of desperation and hopelessness. Gentry had had ample time to come back down and ride away. He hadn't come. And now she was almost convinced that he would never be here.

Still, she wouldn't give in to that conviction. Moving carefully away from the roan she shortly discovered beyond the stall several sacks of grain stacked in a corner. She knelt there and took off her damp shoes. The welcome warmth of the floor's thick cushion of dust soon took the iciness from her feet. And as a growing lassitude settled through her she leaned back against the grain sacks. She was drowsy and for a time tried to keep from falling asleep. But all her senses seemed dulled by the suspense of this prolonged uncertainty, and presently her will to fight the tiredness weakened and she slept.

Much later she abruptly came wide awake. For a moment she was bewildered, not knowing where she was. But then her searching glance picked out the door's rectangle, the blackness there a shade paler than the absolute darkness about her, and she remembered. In that instant a man's tall figure moved soundlessly in through the doorway.

Suddenly she knew who it must be, and a near-ecstasy forced one thankful word from her in an involuntary, hushed outcry. "Dan!"

There was a moment's weighty silence, an awesome one in which Faith was held rigid by a doubt that told her the high shape she had glimpsed might well be Caleb Ash's, not Gentry's. Then suddenly a slow-spoken drawl answered her out of the blackness.

"It's past midnight, Faith. What are you doing here?"

She quickly slipped on her shoes and stood up, a blissful happiness making her want to cry out. And as she started toward him, she softly said, "It doesn't matter. Nothing matters but that you're here, alive!"

"Shouldn't I be alive?"

"Yes, yes! But Ash said you weren't."

Her voice trembled as she spoke and groped her way blindly toward him. The next moment she could see him again silhouetted against the door's faint rectangle. She came in on him quickly and reached out to touch his arm, hungering for the physical proof of his really being there.

"So it was Ash after all?" Gentry drawled, laying a hand on hers. He laughed softly and with a genuine amusement, the sound of his merriment making her want to laugh with

168

him in gladness and relief. "He thought he'd cashed me in?"

"Yes, killed you. And it was —" She hesitated, thinking she was betraying too much of her emotion. But then she added unashamedly, not caring that he should read her feelings, "It was horrible, thinking you were buried somewhere up there."

His hand tightened reassuringly on hers. "Well, now you know how wrong he was. You'd better tell Mike, in case he's wondering."

"He must be. He quarreled with Ash, threatened him."

"So?" There was an edge of cool, quick interest in Gentry's tone. "And did Ash back down?"

"I don't know exactly what happened. I was up there in the room and only heard part of their talk. But Clears finally mentioned a gun and told Ash to get out."

"And I'll bet he got!"

Once again Gentry's low laugh sounded across the shed's dead silence, and Faith, intrigued by this carefree facet of his nature, experienced a moment of sharp regret at the realization that only minutes separated them from a parting that was probably to be forever.

He spoke again now, asking, "Ash knows where the wagons are?"

"Yes. And he's hiring men to dig them out."

"Let him. It's going to cost a big handful of change. Let it be him instead of you."

He took his hand from hers as she told him, "You did what you said you would, gave me the time I need. But if I'd known what was to happen, I wouldn't have let you do it."

"If we'd known maybe we wouldn't have gone at it so fast ourselves," he drawled with a dry amusement. "But no one could have bargained on half the rim falling in. It was a close thing. Ran away with us."

"I don't begin to understand what you did, Dan. You were up there, up above?"

"High up. Working loose a chunk of rock to start things when Ash made his try with the shotgun."

"You're not hurt!"

"No. There was this ledge between us and it caught most of his buckshot. When it finally fell I got out to one side and listened to all the fun going on below. Then right afterward Ash came on up and walked right past me. Ever see a horned toad make himself scarce? I could've reached out and touched him."

"Then everything's all right," she murmured in a voice that trembled with relief. "Waiting for you here so long, thinking that Ash might have been right was like — like last night when I finally understood all that had happened yesterday."

"There wasn't any way down without making a racket," Gentry explained. "Had to climb the rim and then wait up there for things to quiet down. If I'd known you were waiting, I'd have come sooner."

"Of course you couldn't know," she said.

It was then that she sensed how futile these words were, that their talk was merely putting off their parting. It made her uneasy to think that he might sense how reluctant she was to have him go, and now she was trying to find a way of telling him that she didn't want to delay him when abruptly he said, "Up there I got to thinking, Faith. About you. About your having to go out and bring someone in to straighten things out with Fitzhugh. Seems to me there might be a simpler way of going about it."

"What way would that be?"

"That's what stumps me, exactly how to go about it. But there's the Army wire to Denver. Fitzhugh would certainly let you use it."

"But for what, Dan?"

"Getting a full description of you from someone the Department knows in Denver. Or —"

"But Laura Reed was too much like me in looks to have that do any good."

171

"How about a photograph?"

"A photograph?"

"Why not? There must be one among the things in your father's wagon."

She thought a moment. "Old ones, yes. But none recent enough. We did have one taken of the family last Christmas. But Dad didn't like it. He even threw the proofs away and —"

"Wouldn't the photographer still have the plate?" he cut in. "Where was this?"

"In Denver. At a place called The Gallery."

"That's it, then!" he said. "Have Mike go to Fitzhugh and tell him about it first thing tomorrow. Ask him to telegraph Denver. They'll go to this place and have a print made up and send it across here, save you the trip out. If Fitzhugh wants, he could even have it brought across by courier. That ought to wind the thing up in short order."

In this moment as never before Faith was realizing what a debt of gratitude she owed Dan Gentry. To begin with, he had given her her very life. As though that in itself wasn't enough, he had risked his own tonight giving her security for the future where otherwise she would have had none at all. And now as she understood all this a powerful emotion swayed her and she quite deliberately considered something.

Then, because her impulse came from deep within her and was wholly honest, she came closer to Gentry and, tenderly and without reservation, lifted her hands gently to his face and put her lips to his.

His arms lifted, hesitated, then came tightly about her. At once their embrace became a thing she hadn't intended, the heady and exciting closeness of this man awakening a startling and awesome physical hunger in her she had never before known. She had the strange yet absolute conviction that here was the one man who could ever mean everything to her. And now as she felt the desire about to overwhelm her she leaned back in his arms to say breathlessly, "You have more than my thanks for what you've done, Dan. Much more! I wish —"

Her words broke off suddenly as, across the deep regret at his leaving, there struck a thought that made her say in a rush of words, "I'd nearly forgotten! There's something else, Dan. It's — Before you go I want you to know that I don't think of you as these others are thinking. I haven't even from the beginning. And now, just tonight, I've learned how right I was about you. You see, Dan, I know what really happened."

"What really happened?" His tone was unmistakably guarded, and the firm pressure of his arms lightened at her waist. "When, Faith?"

"When you lost your men," she told him. Then, feeling his touch altogether leave her, she hurried on to say, "Mary Fitzhugh told me about it this morning, you see. At first I halfway believed what she said, that you'd disobeyed orders and that perhaps they had a right to do what they did to you. But then this afternoon, getting to know you better, it just didn't seem possible."

She hesitated, considering something that made her ask wonderingly, "Have you ever felt that way about anyone? That you — that in such a short time you can know a person really well?"

"What do you know, Faith?"

The brusqueness of his tone jolted her, made her wonder what she had said that had antagonized him. "That you weren't even with your men when they were trapped in that canyon," she told him. "That you and —"

He suddenly gripped her arms and shook her ungently. His voice grated harshly as he asked, "Who told you this?"

She winced at the tightness of his grip, not at all understanding this violent reaction in him. "I don't know who it was," she replied, her tone awed. "He was someone who came to see Mike Clears right after Ash had gone. But — but what's wrong, Dan? It meant everything to me to hear what he said. Is it something I shouldn't know?"

"It's something no one should know!" He let go her arms, adding in a gentler tone, "Forgive me, Faith. I forgot myself. So Mike knows this?"

"Yes."

He sighed in a way that eloquently expressed his impatience, saying tonelessly, "Then I'll have to go back up there with you and see him."

"But why don't you want this known, Dan?"

"That'd take a lot of explaining," came his enigmatic reply.

She was bewildered, upset by his strange behavior. And as she was trying to think of something to say, he took her arm and drawled, "Let's get this over with," guiding her toward the door.

Outside, as they rounded the shed's corner and started up the alley, he abruptly asked, "Did you think I was leaving for good?"

She looked quickly up at him. "Aren't you?"

"No. Mike decided it was too risky, my staying in town. Because of the chance of Ash spotting me. So I'm headed up into the hills. Mike'll know where to find me."

"Then —"

He must have sensed she was thinking of her having shown her feelings so openly back there a moment ago; for now he told her, "Nothing could drag me away from here now. There's some unfinished business with Ash. I was letting it go. Now I'm going to see if I can track it down. Maybe I'll be helping you at the same time."

His words eased the awkwardness of the moment for her, and he took her arm again, and they went on. Then, as the last of her embarrassment was dying away to leave her thankful and glad once more just to be here with him, he told her quietly, "Some day I'll tell you the whole story about this other, Faith."

His promise of sharing with her something so personal, something she doubted he shared with anyone, seemed to seal a strange and exciting bond between them. She was suddenly glad at having shown him so much of what lay in her heart; and as they walked on his touch on her arm once more roused that strong awareness of him that was so disconcerting but at the same time exciting and welcome.

She was disappointed at their reaching the *Lucky Find*'s alley-platform steps so quickly, at this abrupt ending of the interval that had brought them so much closer to each other. It was as they mounted the steps that he said wryly, "A man's sometimes better off without friends."

She knew what he meant, that he was thinking of Clears. Yet she couldn't help asking, "Where would I have been without friends yesterday and today — without you and Mike Clears?"

"Now you're talking of something else, Faith."

They found Clears at his desk. His head lifted at the sound of the door opening. And as Faith entered the room ahead of Gentry, the saloonman rose from his chair, bursting out in alarm, "Don't tell me you were outside!" Before she could speak, he went on. "Ralph Blake was just here wanting to talk with you. I went up to your room and knocked. Thought you were asleep when you didn't answer. See here, Faith, you can't —"

His words broke off and his jaw hung slack as he saw Gentry come in behind Faith.

"Good Lord!" he breathed incredulously. He grinned delightedly, gladly as his glance shuttled in bewilderment to Faith, then back to Gentry again.

"I know it was wrong to go out," Faith told him. "But I heard what Ash said about Dan. I — I had to know."

Clears was still broadly smiling. "You should have called on me. This town's no place for a woman to wander around alone in." He was still eyeing Gentry in that disbelieving way as he added, "Friend, you really moved the mountain tonight! Ash said you'd come down with it. I believed him. You're a damn fine sight for these tired eyes!"

"What was it Blake wanted?"

The abruptness of Gentry's question made Clears notice for the first time the seriousness patterning his friend's lean face. Puzzled by it, the saloonman nevertheless said warmly, "Ralph was playing a hunch Faith might know something about Shotwell. He hasn't a thing to work on so far."

Faith saw Gentry's glance come around to her. After realizing that he wanted her to answer Clears's question, she told them, "Shotwell kept pretty much to himself. All I know is that he has a wife back in Missouri. He was going back there this summer."

"Blake knows about the wife," Clears said. "He found a letter from her in the poor devil's wallet. But the letter, along with a woman's picture and around a hundred dollars in gold in Shotwell's pockets, is all he has to —"

"Where did the hundred come from?"

Gentry's words, sharply spoken, startled Clears almost as much as his friend's inexplicable seriousness. So now he bridled, "How would I know where it —" Abruptly he caught Gentry's meaning, and his eyes came wider open. He said in an awed way, "Damned if

I'd thought of it! Why would he borrow from me when he had all that?"

Gentry remained silent, and after a long moment Clears asked patiently, "What do you make of it, Dan?"

"Someone got to him before Fitzhugh saw him last night."

"Bribed him?"

Nodding, Gentry drawled, "To lie about the hardware."

Clears whistled softly, eloquently. "Caleb?" When Gentry nodded, Clears asked gravely, "But how do we prove it?"

"Let Blake do that." Gentry spoke with an odd impatience. Then, as Clears was again wondering what lay behind his friend's manner, Gentry said bluntly, "Faith tells me someone besides Ash was down here tonight saying things about me, Mike."

An instant wariness shrouded Mike Clears's expression now as he leaned back against a corner of the desk. And Gentry, after waiting a moment for the man to speak, asked coolly, "Who was it?"

"Ben Qualls."

"How much does he know?"

Clears shrugged. "Enough to make an awful liar out of you, brother! Enough to reopen the courts-martial hearings."

"Get him in here!"

179

"Don't worry, Ben won't talk." Clears regarded his friend in a faintly amused way, shortly asking, "Why in the name o' God did you let them kick you around the way they did?"

Gentry's look was one of unconcealed anger now, and Faith, trying to puzzle out the meaning of their words, knew only that Gentry for the moment seemed on the defensive, an attitude she sensed must be foreign to him.

Then he was saying, a cool edge to his voice, "You've got the name for minding your own affairs, Mike. Don't ruin it."

The saloonman's face reddened. Nodding sharply to indicate Faith, he asked, "Do you want her to hear this? Because I'm going to say some things you won't like."

"Say 'em!"

"All right, here they are." Clears drew in a deep breath, went on. "You're far and away the best man they've ever had up there at the fort. Yet you've let them crucify you for something you didn't do. I'm not going to let it happen!"

"No?"

"No," Clears echoed explosively. "Because I think I know why you did it. You did it for Fitzhugh. Threw everything overboard, ruined yourself to save the feelings of an old man who's damned close to slipping into the

180

grave this very minute!"

Reaching back to his desk, the saloonman picked up a small lavender envelope, gesturing with it as he went on, "Here's proof of that! A note from Mrs. Fitzhugh she sent down here an hour ago. Fitzhugh's had a setback today. Doc Spires doesn't know but what it'll turn into pneumonia. She wanted me to get the word to you if you were still around. Suppose he dies? Where does that leave you?"

Those words had brought Gentry across the room and now he took the envelope from Clears, pulled a sheet of paper from it and glanced at it. The saloonman waited until he was sure Gentry had read the last daintily penned line before he repeated, "Where does it leave you?"

Gentry ignored the question. "This is all you know about the major?"

"Yes." Clears watched as his friend tossed the letter to the desk. Then he said in a gentler tone, "I knew young Fitzhugh, knew him better than I wanted to. He was down here dead drunk more nights than I care to remember. So out on his feet I usually had him carried to that shed out back to sleep it off. To keep his father and that pretty wife of his from knowing what a no-good he was. So someone besides you has tried to save the major's feelings."

Gentry said quietly, "That was white of you, Mike."

"Don't thank me for something I'm sorry now I did, Dan. Now I wish I'd hauled him up there and dumped him on the Old Man's doorstep! Then Fitzhugh would have known what a maverick he whelped. Then you wouldn't have needed to whitewash the lily-livered coward by —"

"No one whitewashed him!" Gentry cut in. "He died with an arrow in his back, died fighting."

"How do you know?" Clears asked intently. "How do you? You weren't even there." He paused; and when Gentry gave no answer, he went on. "It was young Fitzhugh who disobeyed his father's orders, not you. You'd never have taken your men down that canyon when Sour Eye attacked! Would you? Hell, no! They wound up dead because of young Fitzhugh, not you."

"You can't be sure of that," Gentry said. "No one can. Because every man who could tell what happened is dead. All but McCune. And he'd never talk."

"No, Tim wouldn't. Nor can I be dead sure of anything. But I can make my guesses from what Ben found out today." Clears eyed his friend closely. "Where were you and McCune, Dan?"

Gentry's glance went to Faith now and he smiled ruefully as he told her, "You're getting the story sooner than I'd expected." His glance shuttled back to Clears then. "We were there, Mike. But only when the scrap began. Out there on the flats before the column took to the canyon. We'd found ourselves a defensible position, a knoll rimmed with rock. There was even a hollow up there where it was safe to hold the geldings, our own and the new remounts.

"We were holding the 'Paches off nicely when this hunk of lead grazed my temple. That's the last I knew till hours later, after dark. McCune had hid me in between some boulders, had stayed with me on Fitzhugh's orders. We hoofed it into the canyon and hid some more while the hostiles prowled around. Then finally we found the men."

Clears remained silent over a considerable interval, awed by what he had heard. At length he breathed acidly, "So it was young Fitzhugh after all!"

"Yes. He was next in command," Gentry admitted wearily. "He was green, he lost his head. Maybe —"

"He knew his father's orders, didn't he?" Clears cut in. "Knew what a trap that box would be?"

"A man forgets at a time like that."

"The hell he does! Not a soldier!" Clears

glanced at Faith in apology for his profanity before he added disgustedly, "So you took the blame for that yellow-belly's fool mistake!"

"Listen, Mike," Gentry pleaded quietly, "they'd have held an investigation on it anyway. Don't forget, the whole idea of bringing those remounts from Starke was mine. I'd hounded Fitzhugh with it till he had to give in. Remember, he was down sick at the time. And even if Phil Fitzhugh hadn't gone down that canyon, we'd still have lost some men. Probably all our animals, too. It would sooner or later have come out that I was using the Army to work off a grudge against Ash. I was. That meant I was no longer worth my keep as an officer."

"That wasn't it, Dan. You were trying to keep Ash from robbing the Army."

Gentry shrugged and shook his head. "We could argue it all night and never settle a thing, Mike. But I'll tell you this much. When it's — when the Old Man's passed on, they can review the case. Maybe they'd give back the commission and call it quits if I told everything. If I want it, Mike. I'm not yet sure that I do."

"Any day!" Clears said dryly.

"Put you in my place and you'd have done exactly the same," Gentry said. "Just think it over."

"But —"

184

Mike Clears checked his words, glancing helplessly at Faith in the hope she would say something to bolster his argument. But he was jolted to see her staring at Gentry tenderly and in outright admiration. And now for the first time he wavered in his stubborn reasoning, Faith's look making him halfway grasp the logic and generosity of Gentry's act.

So at length he said quietly, "Maybe I understand, Dan. But I'd feel better about it if you'd agree to let me take the whole thing up there after — Fitzhugh's passed on."

"If it'll make you feel any better, I'll agree to do that myself."

"Fine, Dan. Fine!" Clears said with considerable relief. "So you'll hear no more about it from me. Except for one thing. Is there anything I can do now to help?"

Gentry considerd that, finally saying, "If you play this my way, you'll wind up with Ash on your neck."

"What if I do?" Clears bridled. "After tonight he's on my neck anyway. Go on, tell me what you want me to do!"

"You know where I'm going," Gentry said. "You're to keep me posted on Major Fitzhugh, for one thing. And there's something you can do for Faith."

"Name it," Clears drawled.

Chapter Nine

George Spires called early the next morning before Mary had quite finished preparing a tray of breakfast for the major. And presently the way the medico stepped so quietly from Fitzhugh's room, closing the door softly, let her know that the news must be bad even before Spires shook his head and told her in a low voice, "No use in keeping it from you, Mrs. Fitzhugh. He's no better, and he should be."

"You mean he —" She couldn't force herself to voice the thought that struck her.

"I mean he has no strength left for fighting this. There's more congestion, the fever's still high. Have you been giving him liquids?"

"Yes. All he'll take. But he — he doesn't seem to care, doctor. Yet he's cheerful enough."

Spires took his hat from the table and gave her a kindly smile. "Perhaps he really doesn't care. He's been a vigorous man, lived a full life. All this pain and weakness lately can't be much inducement for him to keep on."

"But he can't want to die!"

The medico shrugged. "Who knows? He's lost his son, lost him honorably. And he's lost Dan Gentry, who was next thing to a son to him. He just might be thinking there's nothing much left to live for." With a baffled shake of the head the medico took his hat from the table and crossed over to the door and opened it.

He stopped there in the doorway at sight of Sam Grell turning in off the path. Grell, seeing Mary, saluted before he looked up at Spires to ask, "Any change, George?"

"Not much."

Grell's expression took on a deeper concern. "Will it upset him if I see him a moment?"

"Depends on what you're seeing him about, Sam."

"Some news has come in over the wire. Good news."

"Then see him, by all means. He needs cheering up." The medico nodded his good-by to Mary and went on out the walk.

Grell was ill at ease as Mary silently led the way across the living-room and opened the door to Fitzhugh's bedchamber. But then as he looked in and saw the major lying in his bed propped up by pillows, he forced a smile and went on in, saying in well-feigned heartiness, "Well, sir, they tell me you're licking this thing. Glad to see you looking better."

187

Fitzhugh touched his forehead wearily in reply to his adjutant's punctilious salute. "Take a chair, Captain. Everything going well?"

Grell nodded. "Very well." He waited a moment until he heard the door close behind him, then looked around to make sure Mary hadn't followed him into the room. Facing the other again, he took a folded sheet of paper from his pocket and handed it across. "Here's some medicine that'll do you good, sir. Just came over the wire."

Fitzhugh held the paper in a hand that trembled. As he glanced down at it a look of pleased astonishment came to his drawn features. His eyes were shining with something other than the fever as he looked up at Grell again. "So we've seen the last of Sour Eye!" he said in a voice so low that Grell barely caught the words.

The captain nodded. "The only bad thing about it is that our troops weren't the ones to finish him off."

"Doesn't matter, Sam. Not a whit. What does is that this country can be at peace again. Have you told anyone?"

"No, sir. You and I and the signals sergeant are the only ones who know. I've sworn him to secrecy, as the message requests."

"Good. You'll —"

A sudden racking cough made Fitzhugh choke off his words. He clutched at his chest and leaned sharply forward; and Grell, his look alarmed, stepped quickly to the table and handed the older man a glass of water. Shortly Fitzhugh managed to get down a swallow and then, his breathing rapid and rasping, he lay back once more against the pillows.

His face was darkly flushed, but he managed to get out, "None — no mention of this to anyone, Sam. I —"

After a moment's wait Grell said quietly, "Of course not, sir. We're all confident you'll be back at your desk in a few more days."

Fitzhugh smiled wanly. "Yes. I'll be back." Abruptly, he added, "This comes at an opportune time for us, doesn't it?"

"How do you mean, sir?"

"As concerns our animals."

Grell nodded, understanding now. "Indeed it does. Yesterday I halfway thought of sending a foraging party out for hay."

"I'd suggest you get as many animals as possible up there right away. Today."

"Today?" Grell frowned. "Won't that call for explanations, since we can't let the word out about Sour Eye?"

"Explanations?" The major eyed Grell speculatively, asking in seeming irrelevance, "Would you say that I'd ever used my pre-

189

rogative of playing the martinet, Sam?"

"Never, sir!"

"Well, now I am going to use it." Fitzhugh smiled faintly in a way that let Grell see a spark of the spirit he had once known in the man. "If any explanations are called for, just say that my illness has evidently affected my reason. You may draw up orders for half the animals to be moved up onto pasture in the Box. Assign two good men to hold them there. Sergeant McCune would be one. Let him name the other man."

"A sergeant to work horses, sir?"

"Why not? Might as well make my lapse of sanity look genuine." The older man's smile broadened. "Between the two of us we'll have the whole post guessing."

Grell nodded uneasily. "As you say, sir." He thought of another thing then, continuing, "By the way, Mike Clears was waiting for me as I came on duty. He wants us to do something on behalf of this girl they found in the wagons."

"Laura Reed? What about her?"

"Clears is convinced she's Tipton's daughter. To prove it he wants us to telegraph Denver and have them trace a photograph taken of Tipton's family last year. Have them send it across here."

Fitzhugh was scowling. "Ordinarily I'd be

inclined to trust Clears's judgment. But in this instance he's mistaken."

"So I told him. But he still insists he's right and asks us to help him prove it. I thought it was a matter for you to decide."

The major was studying Grell's expression. "Are you of Clears's opinion, Sam?"

"Not exactly," Grell answered hesitantly. "But Mike seems sure of himself."

Fitzhugh weighed the matter a long moment. Then, with a nod, he said, "Let's prove him either right or wrong. Send the message as he suggests."

By eleven that morning, Caleb Ash had hired his twenty-third man to muck out the rockslide. Satisfied then that he had a big enough crew, he left one of his teamsters to straw-boss the gang and walked on down, crossed the creek, and took a between-buildings passageway to the street.

He almost collided with Trooper Andrews as he stepped onto the plank walk and, reaching out to clamp a hard grip on the man's arm, spun him around to face him.

"Damn you, Andy!" he growled menacingly, "who sent you up to the yard after me last night?"

Andrews tried to jerk his arm away but Ash held it tight, held it with ease. "I — it was just like I said, Caleb," the soldier said uncertainly. "I'd heard they were lookin' for you and —"

"Who said that?" Ash snapped.

It took Andrews only a second to decide to tell the truth. Besides, he thought, it didn't matter now if Ash did know who it was. "Tim McCune," he said.

Ash shoved the man away from him so fiercely that Andrews almost fell. Then Ash asked, "Where's McCune now?"

Andrews backed away a step, thinking Ash was going to hit him. "Up — he left at ten, with a bunch of horses for the Box."

"Geldings, not horses. A cavalryman's supposed to know the difference between —" Ash broke off abruptly, only then realizing what Andrews had said. He asked amazedly, "The Box?"

Andrews nodded meekly, and Ash spoke again. "They've turned animals onto grass up there? With those 'Paches on the loose?"

"Don't blame you for bein' surprised, Caleb." Andrews put a false heartiness in his tone as he stood rubbing his sore arm. "We're all wonderin' if the Old Man's gone loco. But it's a fact."

Ash's surprise had abated somewhat. "They might get away with it if they've sent along a strong enough guard."

"But that's what's got us all worried," Andrews told him. "There's only McCune and one other man up there. Johnny Ewing."

The big man's mouth dropped open in amazement. He shut it again, saying incredulously, "But that's askin' for it! Godamighty! Don't they know what's liable to happen?"

"Makes no difference, I guess. We're short of hay and they had to do something."

"You mean to say they've sent only two men up there to —" Ash was having a hard time taking it all in. "On whose orders?"

"The Old Man's. And Grell's."

Ash shook his head wonderingly. "All I can say is you're liable to be damned short on matched geldings, come tomorrow."

All through the early afternoon that strong chance of the Army losing their animals remained foremost in Ash's awareness. Yet it wasn't until nearly three hours after his talk with Andrews that he was all at once jolted by seeing a startling and intriguing possibility. It came to him so suddenly and so complete in every detail that at first he mistrusted his reasoning. When finally it did dawn on him that his reasoning was sound he was so shaken that he went to his shack, barred the street door, and took a bottle from a box under his makeshift desk.

Standing so that he could see out the window

that looked over the yard and not be surprised by one of his men coming in on him, he took three long swallows from the bottle. Afterward he let his breath go in a scarcely audible whistle that was prompted more by an inner excitement than by the jolt of the whisky.

High up toward the head of one of the canyons to the north of Sentinel, Tim McCune and Johnny Ewing built their supper fire as the twilight deepened. The light of the blaze presently reached out far enough to touch the pole fence running from wall to wall of the deep ravine. From beyond the fence along the foot of the meadow came occasional sounds of the animals moving around through the deep grass.

This had been a confounding day for McCune. He didn't begin to understand why they'd detailed him to this menial duty, nor the reason why they'd detailed anyone. Captain Grell's bland reassurances that nothing would happen to him, that he wasn't to worry, had only deepened the enigma for him. He wasn't forgetting month-before-last's encounter with Sour Eye, nor the strong likelihood that the renegade's scouts were probably right now skulking through the country watching developments at Fort North. In view of that, the very idea of using the Box meadow seemed in itself foolish and

194

risky. The fact of having put out only two men as horse guards made it utterly ridiculous.

But, if McCune questioned the wisdom of the move, he was obeying his orders to the letter. Balancing the seeming absurdity of it, he did have a blind faith in his officers. Robert Fitzhugh he worshiped in the same way Gentry worshiped the man; and Captain Grell he knew to be Fitzhugh's competent, unobtrusive shadow and counterpart. They had sent him up here; therefore it was up to him not to question their reasons.

Only one thing about the day had suited McCune. He'd been allowed to choose the second man; and without hesitation he'd named Ewing. Aside from his misgivings about their being here, he was feeling a grim satisfaction at finally having Ewing to himself. All through the afternoon as they had worked repairing and strengthening the fence, he had planned for the evening, for now. Ewing had complained bitterly over being sent up here. He'd cursed Fitzhugh, Grell, the rest of the officers. Ordinarily McCune would have called him on that. He hadn't. And he'd seen his silence first annoy Ewing, then worry him, until the trooper had finally stopped his raging and ranting and retired into a sullen silence of his own.

McCune had been waiting for the proper

moment to start working on the man. It came now as Ewing, told to throw some wood on the fire, approached the blaze with an armload of split pine. Suddenly and without warning he dropped the wood, wheeled on McCune, and burst out:

"What the hell's the sense of this? Any fire at all's bad enough! You want to build the thing up so's they can spot us ten miles away?"

Something Ewing had said offered McCune his chance. And now he replied quite calmly, but with an edge of scorn in his voice, "If it's comin', nothin' we can do'll stop it, Johnny boy. They probably know already we're up here. So why not make ourselves cozy and enjoy our grub hot while we can?"

"Be damned to your hot grub!" Ewing started toward a near-by log against which lay their bedrolls and carbines. "I'm headed across there to fort up in the rocks!"

"Hold it!" McCune's sharp words stopped the other in his tracks. "The captain said we'd be all right. So I take him at his word and —"

"What else would that bootlicker tell you?" Ewing interrupted furiously. "I claim the Old Man's gone off his head. Grell's just too blind to see it. We stay here and we'll be crow bait by morning!"

"Me, maybe," McCune drawled. "But not

you, Johnny. You needn't worry. You're their *amigo*. They wouldn't touch you."

"Who wouldn't?" An instant wariness settled over Ewing.

"The 'Paches. Who else?" McCune asked blandly. "You did 'em a favor. They don't forget."

Johnny Ewing stood rigid, a look of outright guilt crossing his narrow face. He glanced quickly toward the carbines, then back to McCune again. "What the devil you tryin' to say, Tim?"

"That you passed the word to Ash on the remounts we were bringing from Starke. That Ash tipped off Sour Eye and his bunch."

As he spoke, McCune was calculating the lunge he would make to block Ewing's rush for the carbines. That was as far ahead as he was thinking. He was going to lick Ewing, going to beat the truth out of him.

He caught a rustle of sound behind him and was turning toward it when a voice back there drawled, "Now that's right smart guessin', Tim. Suppose you let me in on it."

McCune swung sharply around. He saw Caleb Ash's massive shape moving in out of the shadows and fear knifed through him. Yet, when Ash stopped several strides away, he managed to put down the fear and ask, "Good guesses, aren't they, Caleb?"

For a moment it seemed that Ash was going to ignore the question. But then the big man smiled broadly, saying, "So long as it's just between the three of us I reckon it won't hurt to tell. Sure they're good. Couldn't be better."

McCune instantly read the threat behind this bland admission. He wheeled. He ran for the log.

Ash's right hand blurred to his belt. He palmed a long-bladed knife from its sheath there without a break in his swift motion. The backswing of his arm and its whiplash forward thrust were a symphony of precise motion.

The knife's blade glinted brightly as it arrowed across the path of the firelight. Tim McCune's catch of breath was almost a cough. His reaching stride broke, he pitched forward off balance and fell in a diving sprawl. His chunky frame slid against the carbines, knocking them from their rest against the log. He lay gasping hoarsely, face down. One clawed and reaching hand closed about the grip of the nearest carbine. His head lifted, then fell back again. And his fingers loosed their grip on the rifle's stock and went limp.

Ewing was slack-jawed, his face gone a pasty gray. And as his terror-stricken glance whipped from the knife handle showing between the shoulders of McCune's sprawled shape, going to Ash, the scout said mildly,

198

"Now Johnny, you just forget what Tim had in mind and do like I say. You and me have always got on fine. Let's keep it that way."

Ewing was visibly shaking now. "But — good God, you've killed him, Caleb!"

"So I have."

Ash spoke with a kind of wonderment. He came across now, reached down, and drew the knife from McCune's back, then wiped it clean on his leggings.

Chapter Ten

Mike Clears left town just past ten the next morning riding Ben Qualls's sorrel mare. As he started up the bench road he was thoroughly enjoying the balminess and brightness of the day, the absence of dust making him hope that summer's long drought was at an end. For the dryness had meant more than a shortage of feed locally. It was, he decided, the primary reason the Apaches had broken from the reservation; for their lands were overgrazed and pitifully short of game. Asking an Indian to get along without meat was merely inviting him to go elsewhere to steal it.

High up near the rim Clears left the wheel

ruts and turned off into the timber, and shortly the mare was wading the tumbling waters of Elk. Three more minutes of deliberate going brought Clears to a break in the pines where he looked across a rock-walled pocket streaked at its upper end by the bright emerald of grass fed by a spring.

He stopped there where the pines gave out, at once puzzled and disappointed. Gentry had been down at the *Lucky Find* last night wanting news of Fitzhugh; here was where he had said he would be this morning. Yet he wasn't here. Clears could see only a ragged short-cropped circle in the grass where an animal had obviously been staked out. And up near the spring was a heap of smoke-blackened rocks. These two unobtrusive signs were all that indicated any man had ever visited the spot.

Warily then he started circling the glade, keeping well back in the trees. Twice he reined in behind dense growths of oak brush to listen, both times hearing nothing but the muted roar of the creek and the gentle sighing of a light breeze through the tops of the highest lodgepoles.

Presently he was close above the spring, the spot where he was sure Gentry must have camped last night. He came aground and, leading the sorrel slowly downward, shortly stood alongside the cold ashes of a fire lying in a semicircle of rocks. A handful of coffee grounds lay in the ashes, and in the dust close alongside the rocks he noticed several tracks made by flat-heeled boots and one clear imprint of the bottom of a fry-pan. It was while he was studying that small strip of ground that his eye picked out some fresh gouges in the black earth.

Squatting there he made out the shape of letters: M . . . IK . . . E . . . TRO . . . U . . . BL . . E . . AB . . . O . . . VE ran the first ragged line. And, below it: AM . . . INV . . . ES . . . T . . . One of Clears's own boot prints obscured the rest, all but the final letter G. *Am Investigating,* was doubtless what Gentry had written last.

The saloonman swore feelingly, taking several more seconds in fully understanding the message. Even as he straightened and turned to swing up into the saddle again, he wasn't sure of anything but that Gentry was away on some obscure errand. *Trouble above* he took as indicating that something had happened on the post; but how Gentry had discovered this was beyond his understanding.

He left the clearing in much more of a hurry than he had come in on it, pushing the mare fast up through the timber, across the creek and then cutting onto the road at a lope. Four

201

more minutes saw him riding in on the fort's main gate. He didn't know the sentry so didn't question him, not wanting to waste time.

He was halfway across the parade, making for Headquarters, when he saw something that, along with what Gentry had said, brought him a strong sense of foreboding. It was Captain Sam Grell coming out of Fitzhugh's quarters and then up along the graveled path at a slow run. Clears had never expected to see the adjutant traveling at any pace other than his usual stiff and precise walk, and the thought instantly struck him, *Something's knocked Sam off his dignity.*

Putting Qualls's mare on at a stiffer trot, he managed to swing in at the tie rail before Headquarters well ahead of Grell. And it wasn't by accident that he stepped onto the path just as the captain came along it.

"What's the hurry, Sam?" he asked as Grell came abreast him.

"Can't explain now." The adjutant was out of breath and at once turned in toward the porch, adding, "Come on in."

Clears followed him into the building, coming through the door in time to hear him telling the sergeant major, ". . . over there and have Moore ask for a repeat on that last message from Starke. Shake a leg, now!"

The sergeant brushed quickly past Clears,

headed for the door. The saloonman took this moment to say, "I can come back later if you're tied up, Sam."

"No, now all I do is wait." Grell gave a perplexed shake of the head. "It's about over, all I can do at any rate. Do things ever pile up on you till you wonder if you're in your right mind?"

"Only in a business way. Which usually means I'm making money."

The adjutant sighed gustily. "Well, this isn't making anything for anybody except trouble. Hadn't even finished shaving this morning when it started. McCune dead, Ewing and the horses gone, the Old Man sinking so fast we —"

"McCune dead?" Clears cut in sharply. "Tim?"

Grell nodded gravely. "Sorry, Mike. I'd forgotten what a friend he was of yours. Yes, I'm afraid he's gone."

"But I was with him only night before last!" Clears protested in a bewildered, disbelieving way.

"It hit me just as hard as it's hitting you, Mike. We don't exactly know what happened. He and Ewing were sent up to the Box with all the animals we could spare. You probably know how short we've been on feed."

Grell lifted a hand to silence the interruption

203

he saw Clears about to make. "It wouldn't interest you why McCune was chosen for the duty. At any rate, a man was sent up this morning to relieve him. This man found McCune lying by his fire with a knife wound in his back. There was damn little else he could make out. All the ground was trampled with hoofprints. He did pick something out of the ashes of the fire, though. It was the head of an Apache war club."

" 'Paches? How could that be? Those outlaws were wiped out 'way south of here day before yesterday. How could it be them?"

A wary, questioning look crossed Grell's face. He nodded slowly. "Yes, we knew that, the major and I. But no one else did. How could you?"

"Ben Qualls was on the reservation two days ago. His friends out there had been talking with their people down south. Smoke talk. The way they got it, Sour Eye was finished, his band wiped out."

"So they were, Mike. But we were ordered to keep quiet about it until they'd rounded up the last few that got away. So —"

"So it couldn't have been 'Paches that got Tim." Anger was crowding Clears now.

Grell shrugged. "Not unless it was a bunch that got away from the fight. I'm trying to get information on that now. A message from

Starke this morning insisted every man in that band was accounted for by late yesterday afternoon, either dead or prisoner."

Clears stood wordless a long moment, then asked quietly, "What have you done with Tim?"

"They're bringing him down now."

"Are you going to do anything about the ones that killed him?"

The grating edge to Clears's words made Grell say gently, "We are, Mike. As soon as we have a thing to go on. Caleb Ash is up there now seeing what he can find."

The saloonman's bewildered, angry look was fading. He shook his head perplexedly, then thought of something else. "You say Fitzhugh's sinking?"

"Rapidly. He's much, much worse this morning."

"Dan'll be sorry to hear that."

"Dan's still around?" Grell was obviously surprised.

Clears nodded. Then, sensing the delicacy of the subject, he asked, "Any word from Denver for Miss Tipton?"

"There is." Grell stepped over to the sergeant's desk and sorted through some papers, at length looking down at one to say, "They've located that family portrait and will send it along next week with the paymaster's detail."

"Which means she waits two more weeks before she knows where she stands," Clears said dryly. "Hell, by then Ash may have the goods sold!"

Grell smiled tolerantly. "You must admit he has a sound claim to them. You can't expect us to have that picture sent across by special courier, can you?"

"Knowing the Army, I don't expect a thing, Sam." Clears's mild drawl took the sting from his words as he turned to the door. Halfway through it he paused to say, "I'd like to know what Ash turns up."

"You will, Mike. I'll send word down as soon as we have anything at all to go on."

"Much obliged." Clears went on out across the porch. He was so preoccupied that he didn't so much as glance ahead until he was halfway down the steps. Even then it was a second or two before he really saw Mary Fitzhugh waiting at the head of the path.

He tipped his hat, said, "Morning, Mrs. Fitzhugh," and went on out to her.

She ignored his greeting, asking, "You are Mr. Clears?" Then, giving him barely time to nod, she asked, "Have you heard about Sergeant McCune?"

"Just."

"Has Dan?"

"Not yet. He —"

"Then he's still here," she said in a hushed, relieved way. And now her look swiftly lost its concern, and her face assumed its striking good looks.

"Yes, he's still around," Clears told her.

"You must tell him that I want to see him before he leaves," she said urgently. "It's very important. My plans may have changed. I want him to know."

"Everything depending on what happens to the major?"

She eyed him closely a moment, trying to decide whether or not his words held a barb intended for her. Then, deciding they didn't, she replied, "That naturally influences my plans. If he — if he passes on, I shall leave, of course. Now that they've rounded up those renegades, the stages will be running again. Would you mind telling Dan that I'll be leaving as soon as I decently can? That if he's going by stage I would like him to wait over a few days for me? I loathe thinking of traveling alone."

"You needn't worry about his leaving right away."

This time the saloonman spoke with an unmistakable edge of dryness to his voice. But she ignored it to ask, "Needn't I?"

"No."

She saw that he wasn't going to enlighten

207

her any further without her asking him to. Yet she was so eager to know what made him so sure of his statement that she put down her pride. "What makes you think he won't leave?"

He smiled faintly. "Just a hunch, Mrs. Fitzhugh. He has a certain interest here. Call it a feminine one."

For an instant his words filled her with happiness. Then suddenly a feeling of dread struck through her, and she was powerless to keep back a question. "You mean the Reed woman?"

"No. I mean Faith Tipton, Mrs. Fitzhugh."

Mary visibly winced. Her face lost color, and a contemptuous look patterned it. "I am aware that you are entitled to your opinion on who she is, Mr. Clears."

Mike Clears acknowledged her remark with nothing but a slight bow, the gesture at once courteous and mocking.

"But I do give Dan credit for having better judgment than you suggest," she insisted.

Her statement had only the effect of making his smile more definite. And suddenly she was filled with a rage so violent that she drew herself up to her full height and, turning haughtily, walked away from him without another word. She had taken but a few steps when she realized the absurdity of parting from him in such a way; but her pride was steel-hard now, and she kept on down the path.

Her thoughts were at a seething boil of uncertainty now, her hopes of the last few days melted away to nothingness. She wanted to cry out against the injustice of what Mike Clears had implied, and in her rage her hands clenched the front of her light wool coat, pulling at the goods until the collar pressed achingly against the back of her neck. No disappointment in all her experience measured up to the overwhelming quality of this one. She felt lost, cheated, and time and again told herself, *He's an evil man! He's wrong about Dan!*

But as she came even with the cabin that had held her prisoner these past three days she knew that Mike Clears could have no reason for deceiving her. Halting at the branching of the path, she eyed the porch door with loathing and revulsion. It seemed impossible that she should willingly submit to going in there ever again and subject herself to the drug-tainted air and the menial drudgery of caring for a man toward whom she felt not the slightest affection. Too many of the major's mannerisms reminded her of Phil Fitzhugh. His kindliness and goodness she had come to look upon as a mockery of her late husband's shortcomings, until she had decided that Fitzhugh pretended to being something he really wasn't.

The sound of the opening of the cabin's door all at once intruded upon her rebellious thoughts now, and she looked across there to see George Spires sauntering out to the porch's edge. He was smiling at her in his gentle way, reminding her of his insistence some minutes ago that she get out for a walk and a breath of fresh air.

Now he called out to her, "Back so soon?"

She squared her shoulders resolutely, wanting nothing so much as to be alone with her thoughts. And quite suddenly the cabin became less a prison for her than a haven, a place where she could be alone. And she walked in along the path, telling him, "I shouldn't have been gone so long," not even thinking as she assumed the cloak of the devoted daughter-in-law, a role she had long ago decided she must play.

"Nonsense. There's little you can do for him now."

The quiet way the medico spoke made her glance quickly up at him. "Has something happened?"

He nodded gravely. "I'm afraid it has. He's in a coma. He may go any minute." He took his watch from vest pocket, looking down at it — "Can you spare me for ten minutes,

Mary? A quarter of an hour at the most. There's a very sick man in the dispensary, and I should be there to treat him. They just sent me word of it."

"By all means go see him."

"You won't mind? I'm sure nothing will happen while I'm away."

"Of course I don't mind, Doctor."

She came on up the steps and he politely held the door open for her, coming in only long enough to get hat and bag before going on out again.

Then, as the door closed behind Spires, all of Mary's worries settled down on her once more. She took off her coat and, her thoughts still a torment, mechanically went through the chores that had so fully occupied her since the major had taken to his bed this last time. First of all she did the breakfast dishes. Then, reluctantly, she went to Fitzhugh's bedroom and filled the pitcher on his bedside table, rinsed out his glass, straightened the sheets and blankets that covered his fevered and now strangely frail body.

It was as she was gently lifting his head, intending to smooth the pillow, that she suddenly became aware of Fitzhugh's sunken eyes being open, staring up at her. For a moment, thinking back on what Spires had said of his condition, she was really alarmed. But then that passed, and she tried not to look at him as she laid his head back again.

Abruptly his weak voice cut across the room's stillness. "Mary, have I ever told you that I'm extremely fond of you?"

She straightened quickly, looking down and studying his drawn face to see if his talk was the unconscious rambling that had kept her awake most of last night, or if he really knew what he was saying. But his eyes seemed alert, and she decided he was conscious. So she forced a smile, telling him, "That's a very nice thing to be saying, Father."

"I mean it, Mary. You are worthy in every way to have been Phil's — his —"

The low note of his voice trailed off and his eyes slowly closed. And Mary, noting his peaceful expression, was suddenly galled at thinking of how utterly absurd and unfair his words had been. In that moment her uncertainties and disappointments seemed unbearable, much more than she could stand.

She stared down at Fitzhugh's sunken face, thinking, *Your loving son! That good and noble man I married! Do you really want to know what he was like, you fool?* And then a host of images passed fleetingly before her mind's eye, and she was once again seeing Phil's sodden contempt for her when he drank heavily, the brutality and meanness in him that had become a part of her everyday life from the moment he had learned he was coming out here. *He was a thorough coward, Major! And he died a coward. Do you hear? He was the most worthless man I've ever —*

She plainly heard the click of the front door's latch, and her rushing thoughts came to an abrupt halt. For a moment as she caught a step crossing the living-room, she felt a stark fear, wondering if she had been speaking aloud, if whoever this was had overheard her.

George Spires came into the bedroom doorway then. He stopped there, not understanding her frightened look. "What is it, Mary? What's wrong?"

And as she stood mute and motionless, too overwhelmed by her emotion to utter one word, he came quickly across to the bed. With a startled look he reached down and closed his fingers about Fitzhugh's wrist, staring around vacantly at Mary a long moment.

Then he straightened and, with a slow shake of the head, said very quietly, "Poor girl. I had hoped to be here to save you this. It must have given you a turn to see the life going out of him."

Chapter Eleven

Looking out over Sentinel's steep slope from a promontory high along its face, Dan Gentry reined in on the roan and paused to watch the last direct blaze of the setting sun lift along the mountainside. His long frame was slack in the saddle, one boot lifted clear of the stirrup and the weight of his upper body leaning on a forearm braced against the horn. He had covered many up and down miles today. Having eaten his last meal at daybreak, the prospect of shortly reaching his camp was distinctly inviting.

This forerunner of twilight laid a hush through the timber, and for a time as he sat there the gradually quieting breathing of the roan was the only sound disturbing the stillness. Then from far below came the muted striking of an ax and, wondering if it came from fort or town, Gentry's glance moved northward until he could see a small wedge of the bench and pick out the log wall of the post.

Abruptly, something he saw down there made him settle more squarely in the saddle.

He frowned, not at first understanding, thinking his eyes were tricking him in seeing the colors, floating lazily from halfway up along the pole that lifted well over the tops of the trees edging this side of the parade. Then suddenly he knew without a trace of doubt that the flag was really flying at half-staff, and he also knew the reason for its being there.

That dread certainty, along with a heavy sadness, was settling through him when all at once the clear notes of a bugle ran up the slope sounding *Retreat*; and, afterward, *To The Colors*. The cadence of the calls were timed slower than he had ever before heard them, as though deliberately wanting to strike a note of mourning. And as he watched he saw the colors dip slowly out of sight behind the solid rank of the pines.

He waited a moment longer before turning downward again, his thoughts remote and very grave. And as the roan took him on down into the trees he was unashamedly and silently weeping.

Ten minutes later and another half-mile downward, when his grief had spent itself; he looked out once more across that lower country and noticed a haze of wood smoke hanging over the break in the timber below. That spot marked his camp. Though he thought he knew the reason for the smoke, he rode on warily.

By the time he looked down through a thicket and saw Mike Clears hunkered alongside a small blaze near the spring, he had regained control of his emotions and was himself again.

The saloonman heard him coming in and straightened, turning his way. And as he came aground beside the fire, Mike Clears studied him closely, at once noticing something in his friend's expression that made him say gently, "So you already know?"

Gentry dropped the reins and stepped back to loosen the cinch, not looking at Clears as he asked, "When did it happen, Mike?"

"Along about noon."

"Was it — how was it for him?"

"The way it should've been. He just went to sleep and didn't wake up."

Gentry's look was unmistakably relieved; and after a moment Clears asked, "How did you know about it?"

"Saw the flag on the way down here."

"Then no one's told you the rest?"

Gentry's glance sharpened. "Is there more?"

Clears nodded. "Tim McCune. He—" Hesitating, not at all relishing this chore, the saloonman went on angrily, "Damn the luck, he didn't deserve it! To cash in that way without a prayer of fighting back!"

216

"Tim's dead?" Gentry's voice was hushed, hollow.

Clears nodded. Over the worst of it now, he explained, "He and Ewing were camped up above in the Box last night. Holding a bunch of geldings. The Apaches caught 'em. They found Tim there this morning. There's no trace of Ewing or the jugheads."

The rock-hard way Gentry's face set made the saloonman add bitterly, "I know what you're thinking. I called Sam Grell on it, told him it couldn't have been Sour Eye. They'd got the same story over the wire yesterday that Ben brought us the other night. Which is why they went ahead and put the nags out. Then today they naturally talked it over with Fort Starke again. Starke claims none of those outlaws got away. But there's the Army for you."

Gentry came in on the blaze now, hands thrust deep in pockets, staring down bleakly at a kettle that simmered at the fire's edge. Yet it seemed he wasn't seeing it. There was nothing Clears could add to what he had already said except a few unimportant details. So the saloonman stood there waiting, letting Gentry think it out.

"I went up there this morning," Gentry said presently, not looking up, "along the hill behind the stables. Just loafin', maybe homesick

217

for a look at the layout. Hadn't been there two minutes when this man busted down the trail to the east gate with his mount damn near done in. Jorgensen, I think it was. Anyway, it looked queer. So I hung around. Couldn't have been ten minutes later when Peebles came out the gate with ten men and went back up that trail fast. It looked like trouble of some kind. So I came back here and tried to leave you word."

"I got it, Dan."

Gentry nodded. "I followed Peebles up there to the Box. Having to keep back out of sight, I couldn't make out much except that Ash showed up after a while and —"

"Grell sent him up there to try and follow sign. It's a serious thing, their losing sixty-four animals."

Gentry looked around. "Did Caleb have any luck?"

"None. He lost the sign along a cut ten miles or so to the north. Said it just played out over cinder rock. There were half a dozen offshoots the jugheads could have taken, and those hills are plenty rough. It didn't rain up there day before yesterday and the wind was blowing, sifting over the tracks."

Now Gentry was regarding his friend in an odd, questioning way. "Caleb lose sign on that many animals?" he drawled. "When I've seen him follow a track Ben Qualls had gone blind on? Hunh-uh!"

"Don't call me on it!" Clears said a trifle testily. "I'm only repeating what Sam Grell told me less than two hours ago. Anyway, Ash couldn't stay away long enough to do a real job. He knew they'd be in a hurry to replace their losses. And he knew he's the only man they can buy from. So he got back down here. He's sending a man out tonight, across to his layout at Taos to have his crew there bring in a new string."

An odd half-smiling look eased the flintiness from Gentry's face. "So our friend Caleb cashes in on their hard luck a second time, eh?" he drawled musingly. "First when I ran into my trouble, now this time."

"Is it Ash's fault he's in the remount business?"

Gentry shrugged. "Guess not." He seemed to catch himself on the point of making some further remark, then squatted on his heels to reach over and lift the lid of the kettle. "Didn't know you were a cook, Mike," he said idly. "What's this we're eating?"

"Something Faith cooked up when she heard I was coming up here." Clears was eyeing his friend closely and after another moment abruptly burst out, "Go on, say what you were going to about Ash."

219

Gentry paid no attention to his words, asking, "How is Faith?"

"Fine. This morning while I was gone she started looking for a place to live. I'd have bet she couldn't find one, but she did. Ralph Blake and his wife have been building a new room onto their cabin. Sarah, his wife, took a liking to Faith right off. She's moved in with them." Clears was silent a long moment, shortly asking, "Now what's this you've got stuck in your craw about Caleb?"

"We were talking about Faith, weren't we?" Gentry looked up guilelessly.

"You know damn well you were ready to say something about Caleb!"

"Was I?" Gentry stood up now and moved on across to the edge of a thorny thicket where he had this morning cached his blanket roll and saddlebags. Although Clears's glance followed him he seemed unaware of it as he took tin plates, cups, forks, knives, spoons, a sack of coffee and a small fry-pan from one saddle pouch and came back to the fire with them. He held the pan out to Clears then, drawling, "If we're going to have coffee we'll need some water."

Clears took the pan and let it hang at his side, asking quietly, "What about Caleb, Dan?"

Gentry eyed him vacantly, a trace of stoniness in his dark eyes as he answered, "I wish I knew. Maybe when I've taken it in about the major and Tim the rest will make sense. Right now none of it makes any. Suppose you add it up and see what answer you get."

"Add what up?"

"Those men that corralled Sour Eye's bunch down at Starke should know what they're talking about. And if —"

" 'Should know' is right," Clears cut in. "Hell, I've seen the Army make worse mistakes than a wrong count on a bunch of shadows! How could they know how many there were? The devils could've had scouts out that missed the fight altogether."

"Then there's the distance," Gentry went on as though he hadn't heard. " 'Paches can cover more miles than a man would dare believe in a day's time. But not that many, not enough to have got back up here from anywhere within fifty miles of Starke by last night. It just isn't possible, Mike."

"Then how could they get down to Starke from where they hit Tipton's wagons? And in almost exactly the same length of time?"

"They didn't," Gentry said intently. "They spotted Tipton's wagons probably the evening before, and probably too late to do anything about it. These 'Paches won't fight after dark. So my guess is they dropped off a few braves to take care of the wagons the next morning. The main band went on and traveled all night, leaving it to the ones behind to catch up later. They were putting plenty of distance between them and the reservation."

Clears frowned, his argument momentarily cut from under him. But then he thought of something that made him insist stubbornly, "All right, maybe some of the young bucks on the reservation got their dander up when they heard what had happened to their sidekicks down at Starke. They busted out, raised their hell up in the Box and're probably back by now with the nags hid and no one the wiser."

"That's possible."

"Sure it is. Anything's possible. Which has damned little to do with Caleb. Much as I hate his gall, I won't see you saddle him with a thing like this without rope enough to tie it on."

Gentry smiled tolerantly but plainly without agreement. "Guess I was looking at it the wrong way, Mike. How about the water?"

Clears knew that nothing he'd said had changed Gentry's opinion on Ash one iota. Yet now he could think of no other argument. Furthermore, he was abruptly feeling he had betrayed something within himself by trying to defend Ash. So, thoroughly disgruntled, he walked off into the deepening shadows to the spring, returning with a pan filled. He set the pan at the edge of the coals, and Gentry silently poured some coffee into it, then filled the plates with the stew from the kettle.

Neither spoke as they began eating. Not once over the next several minutes was that brooding silence broken. Time and again Clears would look at Gentry and each time read into his friend's cold, bleak look that uncompromising certainty of Caleb Ash's guilt.

Gentry was the first to set his plate aside. He rolled up a smoke, scraped fresh coals around the coffee, threw more wood on the fire. Finally he looked around at Clears to drawl with a false heartiness, "Tell Faith I want her recipe. That was plenty good eating. By the way, any word for her?"

Clears nodded glumly and matter-of-factly told of the message Grell had received from Denver. Then, matching Gentry's attempt at levity, he forced a smile and said, "You didn't tell me Mrs. Fitzhugh had gone soft on you, Dan."

There was no break in the look of reserve that had again settled over Gentry's lean face. "Didn't I?" he asked, almost without interest.

"Ran into her up there this morning," Clears went on, wondering why he was even bothering to pass on this information. "She wanted me to tell you she was leaving soon as she can. She wonders if you want to keep her company on the way out."

"What did you tell her?"

"I forget," the saloonman drawled. "Must've been something she didn't like, because she went off in a huff."

Gentry seemed to be already thinking of something else and shortly said, "Makes it rough on Faith, doesn't it, waiting around two or three more weeks."

Clears sighed and shook his head in a baffled way. "Here I try and play Cupid for you, and you don't even listen."

"To what?"

"To what I was saying about Mrs. Fitzhugh. Don't you get it? She wants you to take her out. And unless my guess is 'way wide, it's more than your company she wants."

Gentry's glance fell away. He betrayed nothing but impatience as he drawled, "Have your fun."

"You're not interested?"

Now a faint look of embarrassment did show in Gentry's eyes. "Hell, Mike," he protested uncomfortably, "cook up any story you want and give it to her. Tell her I've already gone if you want. Tell her anything."

"She knows you're still around."

Gentry looked across at his friend with his

glance gone agate-hard once more. "But I won't be by morning."

"You won't?"

"No." Gentry sat straighter. And now as he spoke it was with a deliberateness and a deadly seriousness that backed his cold look. "I'm going up there in the morning, soon as it's light enough to travel. I'll start at the Box and take out on Ash's tracks. I'll go on from where he turned back. I'll stay up there till I find something. When I get back I'll have enough to hang Ash."

Clears shook his head. "You hope."

"I know, Mike. I know! It's there. Something's got to be there. I'll stay till I find it."

Chapter Twelve

Caleb Ash stumbled out of his yard shack and across to the pump behind it that next morning just as the dawn was breaking. Bending over, he worked the pump handle for a solid minute while the cold water gushed over his head. Then, the chill shock having somewhat cleared an unaccustomed thickheadedness, the result of a nearly sleepless night, he went on back in and cooked a breakfast he didn't particularly relish.

He was worried this morning, his mind still tugging at the rather frightening prospect of what the outcome was to be of night-before-last's ride into the hills. He knew all too well the way the Army went about things, the thoroughness with which they would investigate the death of McCune, the days they would spend looking for Ewing and accounting for the whereabouts of every suspected reservation Apache on the night of the murder. Ben Qualls was the logical man for them to pick in getting this information. And Qualls might run onto something, well as he knew the Indians and sure as they usually were of rooting out the facts on anything that concerned them so directly.

Last night Ash's worst scare had come in wondering if he'd left any moccasin prints up there near the fire in the Box where they'd found McCune. Pushing the geldings on down off the meadow with Ewing, he'd tried to drive them across the smoldering blaze, hoping they'd trample McCune's body. But he could still see the way they'd fanned out around the spot or, crowded into it, jumped it and run on. There hadn't been a mark on McCune yesterday, nothing but the stain between his shoulders deepening the blue of his uniform

226

and the yellow of his neckpiece.

This was the worst mistake he'd ever made. And as he realized it he was damning circumstance rather than feeling even the slightest trace of remorse or guilt. It seemed wrong, very unfair, that the cavalry's encounter with the renegades down near Fort Starke had come at such a time as to put the lie to his carefully contrived theft of the geldings. McCune's death would take some explaining in the light of that.

Over his coffee now Ash decided what he must do. It was annoying to have to wait out another hour, until he knew men would be about their morning duties at the post; but he set about killing time. As it turned out he was early even so when he rode in the post gates. He had a twenty-minute wait at Headquarters before Sam Grell appeared.

He didn't waste many words coming to the point. "Now that things are squared away for me down below, I'm going back up there and have another look today, Captain," he told the adjutant. "May be gone three or four days, depending on what I run onto. But I'll find out where them geldings went. And if Johnny Ewing's to be found, I'll be back with him."

Grell nodded pleasantly. "Good. I'll get authorization for your extra pay from Denver this morning. What do you figure your chances are?"

"Damn slim."

The adjutant's look was an understanding one. "Well, do your best. Did you get your man off for Taos last night?"

When Ash had nodded, Grell put another question. "He won't lose his nerve, will he?"

"What about?"

"What happened to McCune."

"I told him the scare was over. He was to make tracks straight across there, fast as he could."

"He's a good man?"

"They don't come any better."

"Fine. Then we ought to see our remounts first thing next week?"

Ash again nodded. "For sure." Hesitating then, he said awkwardly, "You tell 'em why I'm not there this mornin' when they bury Fitzhugh, will you, Captain?"

"They'll understand."

"There went a good man. Good as they come."

"So we all think," Grell said soberly.

As he left the post, Ash was feeling slightly better for having expressed such an honest and righteous sentiment. But then as he swung on into the hills, his worry soon came back again. He soundly cursed his luck in not having heard earlier of Sour Eye's battle with the cavalry from Starke. And he just as soundly cursed Mike Clears and Gentry for having crowded him into making his reckless play; for it had been his doubt about being able to get the wagons out of the cave in time to beat Faith Tipton's claim on the goods that had driven him to make the gamble. It was a gamble he had reasoned would net him even more than the carefully planned steal of the hardware.

Now, and for the first time over these past few successful years, Caleb Ash was actually questioning his motives in taking such long chances to accumulate wealth. Without quite realizing that he possessed an inordinate greed, he knew he had overplayed his hand this time. He would have gladly paid real money, a lot of it, to be able to relive the past two days to a different pattern. There was no remorse in him whatsoever over having killed. It was simply the fact of his killing possibly incriminating him that was the worrisome thing.

By the time he rode his bay horse up on the rail fence in the Box, he was deciding he had still another chore to do today. He would bring Ewing's body in, would see to it that no one with an eye like Ben Qualls found the spot where he'd left Ewing until he had taken care of obliterating all the sign there was that could point to him.

Once he had studied the ground around the fire — and gone back down over the stretch between the fire and where he had tied his horse night before last — he saw how absurd his fears of last night had been. The black topsoil had been so severely scuffed yesterday by boot and hoofprints that hardly a track of his own made the previous night was readable. Even if they had been, he had walked around here yesterday in his moccasins and yesterday's and the night before's sign couldn't now be told apart.

Relieved on this one point, he mounted again and turned back down the canyon, cutting north at the foot of it in a short cut across the thinly timbered hills to the point where he had yesterday turned back on losing the sign. He made good time, and forty more minutes found him casting back and forth across a dry and rocky joining of several finger-canyons that ran along the shoulder of a peak considerably lower than Sentinel, immediately to the south.

There was a choice here — or would have been for anyone but Ash — for this immediate stretch of mountainside was bare and scarred blackly with cinder-hard *malpais,* that honeycombed volcanic rock so jagged and sharp-edged that no animal could cross more than a hundred yards of it without emerging with torn and bleeding hoofs. To any eye other than Ash's it would have seemed impossible for a horse herd to be driven up any of the several offshoots leading to higher country.

All at once Ash was struck by the absurdity of this time wasting, this pretending to be looking for sign when he was interested in but one thing, going straight above to get Johnny Ewing and bring him on down. No one was watching, of course; he could be absolutely sure of that. Yet even as he cut sharply left and angled in toward a hidden trail that led on up through the *malpais,* he scanned the ground as though looking for tracks, that furtiveness in his make-up an unconscious guard against any outright betrayal of the fact that he knew where he was going. And so he followed out the twisting course of that narrow trail up the northernmost shallow, dusty canyon, and in another five minutes was riding the edge of a broad bench that stretched for a good mile back toward an abrupt shoulder of the peak.

He had at first debated on turning the geldings loose right here. For the grass, though brown and very dry in places, was waist-high to a man; and a small pond lay back close to the circling rim that seemed to wall in every foot of the meadow that wasn't guarded by the *malpais.* But in the end he had decided that the risk of the animals being found was too great, for the post lay not quite twenty miles away. So he'd driven the herd on over the mountain, following a trail off the back of the bench that was as hard to find as the one leading to it. Right now those animals must be working their way down off the far east slope toward the plentiful water and grass around Caliente Creek, where they would stay until some stray prospector or Apache ran across them.

It was over beyond the pond where Ewing had made his panicked break and tried to run for it the other night. That had been a close thing for Ash, a hard ride across rough ground in the dark. Even now the scout's pulse quickened as he remembered the long minute he'd had to rein in and sit listening before he heard Ewing's horse thrashing around in the cattails around the small lake's edge.

He was thinking of this, his eye still automatically scanning the ground ahead, when all at once he saw something that froze him in the saddle. The fresh tracks of a shod animal stared up at him, plainly gouged in the black soil and covering the older, dusted-over sign the herd had made coming through here.

Instantly, Caleb Ash dropped to the neck of the bay, sawed on the reins and headed back the way he had come. He didn't draw a full breath until he had dipped on over the bench's edge and was sloping down toward the head of the ravine he'd followed up here. Then, stopping when he was sure he was out of sight of any one who might be on the meadow, he slid from the saddle and took his rifle from the boot.

Less than a minute later his bay horse was tied out of sight behind a cedar, and he was threading his way up through a maze of boulders flanking the trail. He reached the bench's edge a good hundred yards to the north of the trail, where the ravine wall climbed steeply to close off that side of the meadow. From behind one of the many outcroppings along the base of the wall he spent several minutes studying the broad, undulating reach of the meadow. He saw no living thing, not even a bird on the wing. But the back third of the bench dipped away from him toward the pond, and he could be sure of nothing there.

When he moved on he did it quickly, his ability at keeping out of sight uncanny for so big a man. Once a depression near the wall hid him for more than three hundred yards, and he ran most of the distance, crouching as he moved on to higher ground. Beyond, he reached a margin of pines lining the base of the rim. He eased through them at a tireless jog that shortly brought him within sight of the lake and that lower reach of the meadow.

He saw Mike Clears's roan horse the instant the pond's bright reflection came into sight some two hundred yards ahead. The animal was saddled and grazing with reins trailing, standing very close to the spot where Ewing's body should be lying hidden by the tall grass waving fitfully in the unsteady breeze.

Just as his glance had picked out the precise point where he remembered leaving Ewing, Dan Gentry stood up out of the grass there and looked this way.

Ash stood dumbfounded, for a moment hardly believing what he saw. And it was because he didn't move so much as a muscle in his surprise, plus the fact of his buckskins blending with the neutral tones of the ground behind him, that Gentry's glance moved on past the clump of pines and out across the meadow. Ash went flat then, still trying fully to take in the meaning of Gentry's presence here. Only as an afterthought did he squirm closer in to the base of a low-branched cedar and really hide himself.

Gentry stepped over to the roan now, looped the reins over an arm, and led the animal on back to the spot where Ash had first seen him. Only when Gentry had bent down and awkwardly lifted Ewing's stiff shape out of the grass did the scout recover from his surprise and think about moving closer. He came to his knees and crawled on back through the trees, shortly reaching a depression that let him stand. Then he moved on in Gentry's direction, keeping his back to the sheer granite wall.

He had already picked the spot up ahead where he wanted to be. Over the interval it took Gentry to lift Ewing's body behind the saddle, his back turned, Ash made better than half the distance. And each time Gentry stooped briefly to make several turns with the rope he was using to tie on the dead man, Ash worked in still closer.

Gentry was making his last tie to the cinch when Ash finally eased in behind a huge squarish slab of granite some fifteen feet high. It was solid rimrock, a section that had broken loose and fallen from above better than half a century ago. The slab lay in a pocket of the rim's base, a right-angling of the wall where its two joining faces were as straight up and smooth as though finished by a stonemason. There was just room enough between wall and rock for Ash to lie comfortably, his head at the slab's base, his moccasins within inches of the wall itself.

He carefully judged the distance between himself and Gentry, knowing it to be only a trifle more than sixty yards. As he drew back the rifle's hammer he knew he couldn't miss; and the realization laid a slow, pleased smile across his blunt features.

He saw his quarry lifting boot to stirrup now and waited until Gentry had made his ungainly swing up into the saddle, boot lifted high over Ewing's body. Then almost at once the roan was walking obliquely this way. Ash lined his sights at Gentry's chest.

His finger was tightening on the trigger when all at once he was struck by the thought, *Hell, might as well have some fun out of this!*

So he waited until Mike Clears's roan had waded out of the tall waving grass and was walking a comparatively bare stretch before he looked out across his sights again. This time he aimed below the roan's shoulder just ahead of Gentry's shin.

Then, very carefully, he squeezed off his shot.

The shudder of the roan under him and the rifle's flat *crack!* came simultaneously. The reflex that sent Gentry in a headlong dive to his foundering animal's far side was wholly automatic. At the last split second he reached for the Spencer and tore it from the scabbard.

Because the roan was falling, giving him no firm footing, he hit the ground on his knees in an ungainly sprawl. His hat fell off as he

236

was lunging out from the down animal's flailing hoofs, intending to run for the taller grass some thirty feet away. Then suddenly the rifle exploded again, and a hard blow along his right thigh drove his legs from under him. He fell hard, skidding on right shoulder, his face burning against the gravel.

In that instant as he went down the second time, pain knifing sharply along his leg, he knew that he could never reach the cover of the tall grass, knew also that he had never been closer to death than right now. And as that thought flashed starkly across his consciousness, he thrashed violently around, and with a broken, scrambling haste started back for the roan. The dying animal was neighing shrilly, trying to get his forelegs under him. At that threat of losing even this poor sanctuary, Gentry lifted the carbine, thumbed back its hammer and put a bullet through the horse's head.

He threw himself forward then, lunging half the distance that would carry him in behind the roan, now collapsing and stiffening in its death agony. Once again came the brittle bark of the rifle under the rim. Gentry's right wrist, dragging the carbine, twisted with a numbing wrench. The weapon flew from his grasp at the screaming whine of the bullet's ricochet.

He drove himself forward in a final half-roll

that slammed his upper body against the saddle, the roan's bulk finally shielding him. He recoiled sharply as one boot kicked Ewing's bent shape, still securely roped in place. And as he lay there dragging in deep, gasping lungfuls of air against the pain and exertion, he looked back at the carbine lying only ten feet away, wondering what chance he had of going back for it.

He had his answer the next moment as it skidded across the ground to punctuate still another echoing report of the ambusher's rifle. Then, in fast-timed cadence, came four more sharp explosions blended with the whine of ricochets and the metallic ring of lead slamming against the carbine's action. The final blast bore an overtone of jangling metal, and Gentry saw his weapon's action disintegrate, its stock now making a tighter angle with the line of the barrel.

He was badly winded, the torment of his leg putting a catch in his deep, reaching breathing. But now as he sensed how helpless he was without the rifle he felt the prod of the holster along his numbed thigh. He was half lying on it and quickly rolled to one side, drawing the .44 and cocking it, lining it upward against the saddle's swell. He waited that way, tense and wary. He was as ready as he would ever be for what he was sure was coming.

But as he lay there, wincing at the throbbing of his leg, the seconds passed with no sound reaching him to tell him that he was being stalked. And with a faint hope that he might after all be safe for the moment, he edged on back until his head was close alongside Ewing's waist. He raised himself up slowly then until he was looking out through the slit between the body's lashed arm and the roan's sky-pointed flank.

He was peering out past the back of Ewing's blond head at a narrow segment of the rim's base blurred by tall, waving grass. And now he began deliberately searching it, foot by foot, for a glimpse of a man. That man would, of course, be Caleb Ash.

The first conscious labeling of his ambusher came wholly without surprise. Some ten minutes ago, there by Ewing's huddled shape near the pond, he had found one clear moccasin print in the dust, a print big enough to rule out any question whatsoever as to who had made it. Even then it hadn't surprised him to find this unmistakable proof that Caleb Ash was the killer. For the suspicions he had voiced to Mike Clears last night at his camp had strengthened over the intervening hours until finally, accidentally discovering how the horse herd had been driven up through the *malpais* bed, he knew he couldn't be wrong. There were few men but Ash, few Apaches even, who would have known of the narrow trail winding up across that seemingly impassable barrier.

Now Gentry's wary glance pried at each likely spot that might be hiding a man off there along the wall's base. And as the seconds passed without his discovering anything, a strong alarm built up in him until finally it crowded him into calling loudly:

"Try again, Caleb!"

He was afraid that a momentary strengthening of the wind at his back had drowned out his words. Then all at once Ash's deep tones rolled across in answer. "Don't worry! I will, friend!"

A vast relief flowed through Gentry. Here was proof that the scout wasn't wriggling through the grass toward him or circling for another shot. His glance shuttled certainly to the huge slab of rimrock now, knowing that to be the spot where Ash had forted up.

But then his thankfulness became short-lived as he realized how nicely the scout had him pinned down. He couldn't move ten feet in any direction from the roan's carcass without being seen. And he had nothing but the Colt's, a short-range weapon, to match against the uncanny accuracy of Ash's rifle. He knew now that the big man was simply playing with him, knew it because of the ease with which Ash had ruined the Spencer.

As though to point this out, Ash abruptly called out again, "Leg hurtin', Captain?"

Gentry crowded back the impulse to thrust the Colt's in under Ewing's arm and empty it at the base of the granite slab, into the angling of the wall. He would wait, wait until he had something to shoot at before betraying the fact that he knew where Ash was hiding. That gave him at least a slender chance, for the huge chunk of rimrock was within nice range of the .44.

And now it came to Gentry how absurdly simple it was going to be for Ash to pack his body and Ewing's back down to the fort and give a convincing story. He would say he had found the bodies lying close to each other in mute testimony of a shoot-out. He wouldn't have to remind Sam Grell or any of the others who had witnessed the ceremony the other morning that here was a full explanation, along with evidence of a strong motive, for the theft of the horse herd. He, Gentry, had tried to even the score for their taking away his commission. And in his attempt he had done away with his sergeant, who had done nothing to defend him during the courts-martial.

The pain in Gentry's leg was an increasing torment now, and as it burned up into his hip joint he looked down, for the first time seeing the small ragged hole in the denim cloth half a hand-spread above his knee. A dark crimson stain was spreading out from it. Though the leg seemed numb, he could feel a moistness there.

He started to think of what this might mean. Then, wanting to close his mind to that rather frightening possibility, he started pulling his belt from its loops, at the same time looking out through the slit under Ewing's bent arm. He could see nothing in the wall angle or along the base of the rimrock slab. So he rolled over and wound the belt about his leg high in his groin. Then, buckling it, he wedged the Colt's in under it and twisted until he could feel a solid pulse pound that made him hope he had closed off the bleeding.

It was with a panic then that he realized he hadn't been watching Ash's hiding-place for perhaps a quarter-minute. He rocked his head around, caught his breath at what he saw. The scout's arm and one shoulder were show-ing plainly beyond the rock slab's straight inner edge. Gentry's hand stabbed to the Colt's, then abruptly relaxed. For in that in-stant Ash edged slowly back out of sight again.

For a long moment Gentry felt weak and completely defeated at realizing what a chance he had missed. But then came the faintly heartening realization that Ash might purposely have exposed himself and, his move not having drawn a shot, that he might grow careless now. Though he had undoubtedly seen the Colt's, he might be deciding that Gentry was too badly hurt to defend himself.

Everything depended on making Ash think he didn't have to be careful. So now Gentry put a deliberate break in his voice as he shouted weakly, "Caleb, I'm — sure of one thing. You were in with — you rigged that tangle with the 'Paches when I lost my detail. But what about Tipton's — his wagons being caught? Did you pass the word to Sour Eye on that, too?"

Watching the wall corner, Gentry saw Ash's right hand move suddenly into sight beyond the edge of the granite. He started reaching for the .44 again. Yet, hoping for an answer, he hesitated in drawing the weapon and lining at this poor target.

Ash's answer came then, his deep tone nearly smothered by a strong gust of wind. "Save your breath, Captain. You'll need it!" And as he spoke the big man's hand moved slowly back out of sight.

The arrogance and sureness of those taunting words roused a fury in Gentry that made him fist a hand tightly about a clump of dried grass alongside his bad knee. Savagely, he

243

pulled the roots from their poor anchoring in the dust. Then, about to toss the grass aside, he looked down at his hand wonderingly, his rage slowly subsiding before a strong lift of hope.

Why didn't you think of it before? he asked himself. And quickly then he reached to a shirt pocket with his other hand and took out some matches. He laid the matches close beside him and began pulling more grass. Every few seconds he would turn his head and look back into the wall corner. And now a strong excitement eased the lines of pain from his lean face; he was almost smiling.

Finally he had pulled as much grass as he could hold wadded in one hand. He lay back then, struck three matches at once, and lit the ragged ends of the bundle. The dry blades blazed up fiercely at first. Then as they were dying the thicker matting caught, and shortly one whole end of the bundle was alight.

Gentry rolled onto his back and pitched the grass out over Ewing's bowed body in Ash's direction, well beyond the carcass and downwind. Then he pulled the Colt's from the belt twisted about his leg, thrust it in under Ewing's arm and waited.

Hardly had he gone motionless when he felt a strengthening of the wind at his back. Several tongues of flame were licking upward through the thick grass some ten feet away. The wind was fanning the blaze, sweeping it out from the carcass toward the wall base. And as thick curls of smoke lifted up out of the grass, he thumbed back the hammer of the .44 and aimed into the angling along the walls.

He had no sure target; he was gambling on a ricochet, on his bullet glancing off the wall toward the spot where Ash was standing.

The gun exploded and bucked sharply against Ewing's stiff arm. Hard on the heels of that first shot, Gentry threw another. Over its thunderclap echo he caught Caleb Ash's startled outcry. He was lining the Colt's once more when he saw the big man's left shoulder appear abruptly beyond the far side of the granite slab.

He brought the .44 around and squeezed trigger. He saw his target jolted back at the bullet's impact, and he savagely tried to throw another shot. But Ash's lunge for cover came too soon.

Now he rolled onto his side and reloaded the Colt's, excitement welling up in him at realization of the luck that had backed his gamble. His lead had either hit Ash in glancing or had come close enough to panic the scout into momentarily exposing himself. And there was no doubt about his third bullet having found its mark.

Out ahead of him the smoke-fog thickened now until it was hard to make out the detail along the wall's base. He pushed the Colt's under Ewing's arm again. The next moment he recoiled violently and dropped face down to hug the ground as the trooper's body jerked at the flat report of Ash's rifle. Pain stabbed along his bad leg as he wormed his way on back to the hindquarters of the carcass. But he ignored it, warily peering out past the roan's rump, laying the .44 in line with the boulder once more.

A band of leaping flame was now crawling away from him toward the base of the wall, a cloud of smoke hanging over it so thick that he could no longer make out the slab of rim-rock. But he well knew exactly where it lay, and now he threw three fast-timed shots into the wall angle. He was rolling back behind the roan before the *crack!* of Ash's rifle came again, the bullet striking the carcass with a muffled thud.

He moved fast now, lying flat while he thrust the .44 in under the belt at his leg again, then getting to his knees. He began crawling away from the roan, keeping the carcass in line with Ash's rifle and favoring his bad leg as best he could.

Once more during those first few seconds as he was moving away the rifle spoke loudly, menacingly. It was that sharp explosion that made Gentry abruptly angle out from the line of the carcass. A backward look showed him the foot of the rim still obscured by smoke.

When he had gone a hundred feet on back toward the pond, he was finally hidden by the taller and thicker grass. Breathing heavily, he paused there and quickly set fire to the grass, having to move on hastily as the flames caught and fanned quickly out to either side of him. Then when he was deeper into the tall grass he stopped and lay down, giving in to a lightheadedness that suddenly hit him.

Going on presently, he ran in a broken, painful stride that put a catch in his breathing. In another half-minute he had the sound of one more rifleshot to bolster his hope and quicken his lurching stride. When he heard it he quartered around, now running to the edge of the bench that dropped down into the *malpais* better than half a mile distant. And he was wondering how long it would take Caleb Ash to become suspicious, risk the threat of the .44, and circle on out beyond the grass fire to see that he no longer lay behind the carcass.

If he could reach the draw that led on down off the bench he knew he would have a better than even chance of hiding himself so that Ash would never stalk him. That was as far ahead as he would let his thoughts go. How he was to get down out of the hills was something he would think about when the time came to do it.

He was weakening fast now. The distance he could cover before having to stop to rest grew shorter each time he moved. Always as he paused to catch his breath he was looking back toward the two pluming lines of smoke beyond the wall. And when he finally saw Ash's tall shape suddenly appear out of the blue smoke-fog well above the spot where the roan lay, well beyond the pond, he felt a relief rather than surprise. For then the certainty that he had a chance replaced the mere hope of one.

When he first saw Ash the man was a good six hundred yards away. And he wasted almost a quarter-minute watching the scout crouch and, half hidden by the grass, start circling in on the spot where the roan lay. That proof that Ash hadn't yet guessed his maneuver brought a gusty, delighted laugh welling up out of his chest. He turned away then and, hunched over so that the thinning grass almost hid him, plodded on.

The next time he stopped and looked back, almost a hundred yards beyond, Ash was out of sight. When he had caught his wind, he came tiredly to his crouch once more and set his mind to the torment of easing his weight onto his bad leg for the briefest possible time necessary to take a step in that stooped attitude. He had discovered the knack of throwing the weight of his shoulders into his lurching stride so as to drag the leg pendulum-like and not bend his knees. The knotting of the thick muscle along his thigh against the pressure of the crude tourniquet was the most painful thing of all; and during his more frequent halts now he stretched the leg out straight and took the .44 from under belt. The relief each time he did this was so keen that it seemed to outweigh the danger of the loss of blood it cost him.

Finally he was within sight of the head of the draw, only a hundred yards short of it. He was plodding along wondering how many more steps he could take before having to rest again when suddenly a feathery air-whip touched his face. He dropped in his tracks. Looking quickly back toward the pond as the hollow *crack!* of the shot reached him, he saw Caleb Ash coming at a jog little more than two hundred yards away.

His first instinctive move was to reach for the Colt's. He didn't complete that gesture, at once realizing that Ash was too far away for even a lucky shot to have any effect. As he lunged to his feet, he had a moment's grim satisfaction at seeing the loose, crippled way the scout's left arm was hanging. He took several stumbling steps obliquely to his right and afterward cut quickly to the left. He forgot everything but the threat of the rifle, of his life being balanced against Caleb Ash's skill with the weapon.

The knotting of the muscle in his groin now made him pull the .44 from belt. Afterward, with the bad leg suddenly able to bear his weight, he made his side-to-side run almost without a break in stride. The rifle slapped sharply once more, but he had no knowledge of where the bullet went.

He reached the head of the draw and the shallow wash flowing into it quite unexpectedly. And as he vaulted from the bank, the angry whine of a bullet punctuated the painful shock of his leg catching his weight, then buckling. He fell in an instinctive roll that carried him to his feet again. As he turned on down the wash, he looked out over its edge and saw that Ash had halved the distance separating them. So, with his breathing crowding him unbearably, he suddenly halted, lifted the .44 and began firing.

The thunder of his four deliberate shots was rolling away across the bench when he caught the break in Ash's hurrying stride. The big man stumbled sharply to one side, then went to his knees. He didn't go all the way down. Instead he lined the rifle. And now as his crippled left arm hung at his side and he leveled the weapon with only one hand, Gentry understood why those other bullets had been wide of the mark. Ash couldn't use his left arm. Even so, Gentry hunched over and waited until the bullet had snapped overhead before straightening to go on, the rifle's report coming as he moved.

The wash tilted steeply downward now, and Gentry had his first good look at the twisting ravine directly below. His eye was shuttling quickly from one spot of cover to another, trying to decide on one, when suddenly he saw the hindquarters of Ash's bay horse showing beyond a cedar only twenty yards obliquely downward and to his left.

For a moment he could scarcely believe what his eyes were showing him. Then, awkwardly scrambling up the wash's far bank, apprehension thinned his lifting hopes. A backward look showed him that Ash hadn't yet reached the bench's edge. But as he plunged on he knew that he had at best a respite of only a few more seconds.

He weakly stumbled and half fell into the cedar as he finally ran in on it. With a fierce tug at the reins, he pulled the knot loose and tried to step in on the bay. The animal kept

shying away, tossing his head. Gentry shortened his grip on the reins and looked back
once more. He saw Ash's big shape suddenly
sky-lined, looking down at him across a distance of perhaps eighty yards.

With his gun hand putting a steadying pressure on the reins that took all his remaining
strength, Gentry eased around and managed
to get a hold on the horn. It was more than
he could do to lift boot to stirrup. So, with
a vast effort, he heaved himself up and went
belly-down across the saddle as the bay shied
violently away. The animal was making a panicked wheel outward from the cedar when the
sharp report of Ash's rifle rode down the draw.

The bay stumbled, the abrupt change of
weight helping Gentry lift a leg over the high
cantle. For a moment it seemed that the horse
would go down. Gentry knew certainly that
the animal was wounded. And as his boots
found the stirrups he hauled the bay's head
up savagely and reined him on away. Somehow then the animal found its stride and
lunged into a hard run.

Gentry turned in the saddle now and laid
the .44 in line with Ash. The scout's rifle was
lifting again. There was no way Gentry could
steady his weapon, and with a stark dread he
realized that he hadn't reloaded in his headlong flight down from the head of the ravine.

Yet he took what care he could with that one remaining bullet, firing as he saw Ash's rifle settle into line. Then immediately he pulled the gelding around in a change of direction.

He saw his bullet kick up dirt several feet to one side of Ash. He saw flame stab from the rifle's muzzle squarely at him. He felt a tug on the reins. Glancing quietly down, he saw the left rein dangling loosely from his hand, a foot of its other end flapping from the bit.

Bracing himself in the stirrups, he leaned down alongside the bay's neck and snatched at that broken rein, caught it. But he couldn't straighten again, and from this awkward position he tried to look back.

All he could see was this lower reach of the ravine with its steep near slope crowding closely in from the left. Ash was beyond his line of vision. That knowledge turned his long frame rigid, expecting to feel the slam of a bullet at any moment. Then another thought made him drop the severed rein and straighten in the saddle. Wonderment was in his eyes as he glanced back there once more.

A turning of the depression had hid the bench's edge. He was away.

Chapter Thirteen

They buried Robert Fitzhugh at eleven that
morning. Mike Clears attended the services.
He stood apart from the others, close to the
gate in the cemetery's rock wall beyond which
he had tied his borrowed buggy. And the cyn-
icism in him was utterly gone before the im-
pressiveness of the ceremony.

The troops were drawn up in double lines
facing each other across the mounded earth
of the open grave. Lieutenant Peebles had
led Fitzhugh's sorrel, stirrups tied across the
saddle, to one end of the grave close to the
flag-draped casket. Mary Fitzhugh, Sam
Grell, George Spires, and the other officers
stood opposite. And in watching the young
widow, Clears noticed the way she finally
lifted her veil and stood with head bowed, a
handkerchief held to her eyes. He revised his
opinion of her somewhat then, putting aside
his impression that her nature was too calculating, cold.

After George Spires had spoken his solemn,
reverent words, half a dozen men of each troop
dismounted and came to either side of the

grave with their carbines. At Peebles's command they presented arms, loaded their pieces. Then they brought them to shoulder and fired two crisp volleys that rolled sharply up the timbered slope beyond the log wall.

The muted rattle of those shots reached Dan Gentry two miles away and far above. And on hearing them he straightened from his slouch with a vague alarm stirring him out of his pain-dulled apathy.

After that first panicked, headlong run down to the head of the twisting trail through the *malpais* an hour ago, Gentry had pulled in on the bay and managed to tie the broken rein. At that slow pace the animal's stride had developed a decided limp. So, on the way down through the *malpais*, Gentry had leaned out from the saddle and looked down until he found a bleeding, ragged tear in the skin along the thick-muscled gaskin of the bay's left rear leg.

The wound was painful but not dangerous, he had decided. His lightheadedness and a fresh moistness along his thigh warned him that time was the all-important factor now, that he couldn't help the horse. So he had gone on, working the .44 in under the belt at his leg once more.

As the miles dropped slowly behind, he stopped thinking back on what had happened, stopped thinking of much of anything. The insistent pound in his groin would from time to time grow unbearable. He would lift the Colt's out then until the pain slacked away. Though the stain above his knee would turn a brighter red each time he did this, he knew he had no choice; not only was it impossible to stand the pain, but he remembered having once heard that to keep the flow of an artery shut off completely was to risk gangrene.

The bay was traveling steadily downward, seeming to be heading for its home corral. Once he was sure of that, Gentry had relaxed his vigilance to the point of dozing when the pain would let him. But now as those two widely spaced volleys alerted him, he looked around and saw that he was crossing a familiar, narrow meadow where Elk Creek flattened out after its precipitous fall off the side of Sentinel. And suddenly he was feeling a powerful thirst.

He saw a low outcropping ahead and reined over to it, stopping the horse alongside and stepping out of the saddle. He managed with some difficulty to slide on down to the ground. Then he led the bay across to the stream, only ten yards distant. There he lay and put his face into the water, gulping down many full swallows and only at the last moment remembering to stop the horse from drinking its fill. Momentarily refreshed, he plodded on back to the outcrop, climbed it and went astride the saddle once more.

This effort left him dizzy and weak, gripping the horn to keep from falling. When the bay started on before he intended it, he had several bad seconds when he was sure his stomach was refusing the water. Then, gradually, his awareness settled back into that twilight somewhere between consciousness and delirium, the throbbing along his leg the one thing that gave him even a slender hold on his reason.

His next fully conscious moment brought excruciating pain and a surprise. The bay was taking him along the lower reach of the road down off the bench, and he had a bad moment before he realized he was well below the post. He quickly drew the .44 from his groin; and as the pain receded he found he could no longer push himself straight but had to sit hunched over, holding to the horn.

He met no one along the road. At the foot of the bench the bay turned without the rein up past the nearest placers and into the foot of the alley. It was about a hundred yards now to the *Lucky Find*'s rear platform, and as the crude shacks and cabins fell behind, one by one, Gentry began wondering quite lucidly if he could stay in the saddle as far as the saloon. The thought of the surprise he was bringing to Mike Clears made him smile crookedly in pain.

He wondered, too, if Faith would be there, and it irritated him to think he was forgetting something Mike had told him about her last night. *That was a long way back,* was his thought as he remembered his talk with the saloonman there at his camp by the fire.

Thinking of Faith he was drowsily startled now to hear her voice sounding dully across his consciousness. He liked the tenor of her words, which he hadn't caught. And as she spoke again, saying quite plainly, "Dan! Stop!" he wondered what fragment of circumstance he could be imagining.

Then abruptly the motion of the saddle beneath him ceased altogether. His glance shuttled outward from its sightless concentration on the bay's mane, on the swell of the saddle. He found himself staring down into Faith's uplifted, frightened face.

He realized then that this was no dream. Her eyes were wide, afraid. She was holding the reins tightly with one hand, reaching up to him with the other as she breathed, "My dear, you're hurt!"

He tried to smile, to shake his head so as to ease her worry. He looked on out past her to see that the bay stood close to the picket fence at the rear of Ralph Blake's slab cabin.

Now he remembered what Mike Clears had told him last night. Faith had moved in with the Blakes and was living in the new room.

Just then she startled him by calling, "Sarah! Come help! Hurry!" and he glanced over to the cabin again in time to see Blake's wife come running from the kitchen door. He sat straighter now at the risk of losing his balance. And as he swayed uncertainly, Faith took his hand and said gently, "Get down, Dan. I'll help."

He was so delighted not to be imagining all this that he stared down at her with a broad grin. "Got some things to tell you, Faith," he said huskily. "Some things you'll be glad to hear. Just —"

"Just don't try to talk now," she told him as his words trailed away. Her frantic glance was pleading with him as she added, "Can you help us get you down?"

Very deliberately he let go the reins and tightened his grip on the horn. Bending at the waist, he lifted his good foot clear of stirrup and, trying to hold his weight, slid down off the bay. He would have fallen but for Faith and Sarah Blake holding him erect.

Faith drew one of his arms about her shoulders and Sarah Blake took the other and they led him awkwardly on in through the gate and up to the kitchen door. It took a definite strength of will for him to manage the two steps, to keep from tripping. He was breathing hard and loudly as they helped him across the kitchen and into another room.

He saw a bed there. They led him to it, and he sank upon it with a groan of relief. Then, as Faith lifted his boots onto the blankets and he stretched out full length, he gave up trying to keep his eyes open and fell at once into a deep sleep.

Chapter Fourteen

Gentry came starkly and completely awake at a scalding pain along his leg. He was instantly aware of a weight at his chest. It held him down tightly, and as his eyes came open he was thrashing and crying out hoarsely.

First of all he saw Sam Grell's head and shoulders braced solidly above him. Grell was sitting on his chest, had his arms pinned down with knees and hands. And in sheer agony Gentry caught his breath, lifted his head, and stared wildly about him.

He was in a small room, lying on a bed. Something was gripping his feet tightly; and with the easing off of the staggering pain, he let go his breath in a groan that brought George Spires's head into sight above Grell's outline.

"Sorry, Dan. But we had to get this corruption out," the medico said. "Can you take more of it?"

Understanding now what was happening to him, remembering his bad leg and how he came to be here, Gentry's reeling thoughts steadied enough to let him answer, "Go ahead. But get it over with in a hurry."

Before that second blazing stab of pain hit his right side, Gentry briefly glimpsed Mike Clears peering worriedly at him from the foot of the bed, which meant that it was probably the saloonman who was holding his feet. Then he caught his breath again, closed his eyes, and his long frame tightened rigidly against more of the torture.

"That does it," finally came George Spires's words.

Gentry lay there limp and with eyes closed as that excruciating pain eased slowly away. He felt Sam Grell's weight leave his arms and chest, the bed sagged, came even again. And then abruptly a cold cloth was gently stroking his cheeks and forehead, wiping away the dampness there. He opened his eyes and found the pale beautiful oval of Faith's face close above his.

He smiled up at her in thanks. And the tenderness that touched her glance then, the gladness of her answering smile, was so eloquent that suddenly and without the trace of a doubt Gentry knew that he loved the girl.

His eyes must have betrayed this startling awareness. For all at once her look took on a wondering, rapturous quality that made him forget the pain, everything but a powerful longing to share with her this new-found realization.

"Better, Dan?" she asked after that long moment when their eyes had so mutely bared their innermost thoughts.

He tilted his head in a weak affirmative and he watched her straighten self-consciously and step aside. That let him see the others, Mike Clears standing there at the foot of the bed grinning relievedly, Spires bent over a table beyond, lathering his hands in a basin of steaming water, Sam Grell shrugging into his tunic and looking down at him apologetically.

"No hard feelings, Dan?" Grell asked in all seriousness.

Here was the old Sam Grell, the friendly, somewhat shy man so unlike the indignant and offended adjutant who had spoken his mind so openly at the ceremony the other morning. And Gentry drawled, "Not a one, Sam," meaning it.

The sound of Gentry's voice brought Spires across from the table to stand alongside Clears. He was wiping his hands with a towel, and his look was one of sober amazement. "You're tougher than any man has a right to be," he said. "Feel like talking?"

"What about?" Gentry's voice was gaining firmness.

The medico's head tilted to indicate Clears. "Faith sent Mike up after us. On the way down here he told us some things that're hard to believe. On top of that we find you with a hole through your leg and forkin' Ash's horse. What does it all add up to, Dan?"

Gentry lay a moment wondering what to say, where to begin. Then, wincing at the tenderness of his leg, he got his elbows under him and pushed up so that his head and shoulders rested against the iron bars of the bed's head.

He noticed for the first time that he still wore his clothes. The right leg of his waist-overalls was slit along the outside seam from ankle to hip; although he hadn't felt it, Spires had wound a broad bandage above his knee. His upper body was still damp from the punishment he had taken, and he could feel his arm muscles quivering as the nerve strain gradually eased away.

He made an automatic gesture of reaching

to his shirt pocket. His tobacco wasn't there, and he realized he'd probably lost it somewhere up along the meadow where Ewing and the roan lay. It was Sam Grell who noticed the gesture and quickly took out his own tobacco, passing it across and saying, "Here, smoke mine."

Gentry began building the smoke, still wondering how to begin telling all there was to tell. And in a few more seconds Grell helped him again. "Maybe we'd better ask our questions and let you give the answers, Dan." He waited for Gentry's nod, went on, "Mike says it was Phil Fitzhugh, not you, that took your detail into that canyon. He claims a bullet had grazed you alongside the head, that you were knocked out. I can remember your head was bandaged for several days. Is what he says true?"

Gentry's glance shuttled quickly around to the saloonman in such an accusing way that Clears blurted out, "I know! I've broken my word. But a man can stand so much, Dan. I won't see you go through with this now that there's no need to."

Spires spoke then. "Is that what really happened, Dan?"

Gentry sighed gustily. "Yes, that's what really happened."

The medico and Grell looked at each other

in surprise, and it was finally Grell who asked, "Then why — How come McCune didn't give it away?"

"Because I made him swear to back my story." Gentry had lit his smoke now and drew deeply on it, fixing a glance on Grell that was angry, uncompromising.

"You did all this for the Old Man, of course," Spires said gravely.

Gentry shrugged. He was running a hand along his bad thigh as he drawled, "That part of it, yes. Why else, George?"

Faith, standing in the doorway near the head of the bed, said softly, "Dan, Major Fitzhugh's gone now. You needn't hold back any longer."

Looking around at her, Gentry laughed softly, scornfully. "You don't know the Army, Faith. Let 'em get their teeth into this thing and they'll smear the name of Fitzhugh till every friend the Old Man ever had will —"

"Doesn't that depend on me?" Grell cut in quietly.

Gentry looked across at the man coolly, speculatively, in a way that made Grell add, "Give me credit for having some feelings, Dan. You and McCune lied under oath to keep from hurting the major. So I can stretch a point or two in my report, can't I? By just omitting any mention of Phil Fitzhugh knowing anything at all about his father's orders on avoiding that canyon."

Some of the severity eased from Gentry's expression. "That would certainly help."

"Now about this other," Mike Clears said, his relief quite obvious. "Your hunch on Ash must have proved out."

"It did, Mike."

At the puzzled looks of the others, Clears explained, "Dan was blowing off steam against Caleb last night. He's had it in his craw all along that Caleb could have tipped off the 'Paches about those jugheads being brought up here from Starke. That it was because of him Sour Eye wiped out your men."

He lifted a hand, cutting short an interruption he saw coming from Sam Grell, hurrying on to say, "And Dan had another hunch I combed him over for. With those outlaws all either dead or corralled down by Starke the other day, he had the idea maybe it was Caleb that ran off your geldings and cashed in Tim McCune." His glance swung across to Gentry now. "Was that the way it turned out, Dan?"

Gentry shrugged. "All I know is what I found up there today. First, Ewing. Dead. All around him there were tracks. Moccasin prints that had been there as long as he had, at least a day and a night. They were big. They couldn't have belonged to anyone but Ash. And Ewing was shot in the back."

It was a long moment before any of them could speak, and it was George Spires who breathed, "Good Lord!"

Sam Grell finally found his voice. "You're saying the man would murder, kill twice, to turn a few dollars?"

"Not only twice, but he tried to make it three, Sam." Gentry lifted a hand and, with his thumb, tapped his chest.

Clears asked, "Where is he now?"

"Still up there. Afoot and with a hole through his shoulder."

Sam Grell was shaking his head with a look of complete bewilderment. "This is almost too much to take in. The man must be insane!"

"Did he — did you get to talk with him, make him admit anything, Dan?"

Gentry smiled thinly. "Not a thing, Mike. All we can do is guess. And so long as we're doing that, here's one to think over. If he threw in with the 'Paches once, he could have done it twice." He looked around at Faith. "We know he lied about the hardware, stuck to his lie even after you'd been found. That looks to me like he'd planned it beforehand."

Sam Grell asked sharply, "You're saying he had Tipton's wagons spotted for Sour Eye, Dan?"

"We were guessing, Sam."

267

"How could that be when Tipton's man backed Caleb's story on the hardware?" George Spires wanted to know.

It was Clears who answered, "We know for sure that Shotwell took a bribe, lied about that hardware. And now it's not too hard to believe Ash killed him to keep him from ever talking."

"Don't make it any worse than it is, Mike." Grell was eyeing Gentry then as he asked, "You're sure about those tracks being Ash's, Dan? They couldn't have been 'Pache?"

"They could've been if you can find one with a foot as big as Caleb's. Which you can't." Gentry looked at Clears, adding, "By the way, Mike, I lost you a good horse."

Grell put in impatiently, "Tell us where Ash is, Dan. We'll go up there and bring him in."

"I can tell you where he *was*. But that won't help. Too much like chasing a shadow. If you want him, put some men in his yard here in town and wait for him to show up tonight."

The adjutant's glance was puzzled. "You don't think he'd come back here again with what we know about him now?"

When Gentry nodded, George Spires scoffed. "Not a chance, Dan. He'll travel just as far from here just as fast as he can."

"You're wrong, George. He's made money, a lot of money. He's cached it somewhere on his layout and he won't leave without it. He

268

killed for money, didn't he? Killed more than once, even turned against his own people. So he'll be back for the stake he took all the pains to collect. Tonight probably."

Grell shook his head. "I don't agree. George is right. If Ash is guilty of half the things we think, we'll never see hide nor hair of him around here again. I'm going to send Peebles up there where you last saw him and track him down. It'll be a duty Peebles will relish, by the way." He glanced at Faith, adding, "Our green new lieutenant is already regretting his part in helping Ash convince the major you were Laura Reed, Miss Tipton. He mentioned it to me today. Said you were too nice-looking ever to be trying to rob anyone."

"Even supposing Ash doesn't come back," Gentry insisted impatiently, "you'll never find him, Sam. If he's heading straight out he's probably already caught up one of those geldings he ran off the other night. So your only bet is to wait for him down here."

"Just where did you leave him, Dan?"

Gentry sighed his exasperation, then grudgingly described the location of the *malpais* bed. But he finished by insisting, "I tell you, it's a waste of time to look up there."

"We'll see." Grell's tone made it plain he wasn't convinced. Gentry was about to protest further when the adjutant all at once came to the side of the bed and thrust out a hand, saying gravely, "Can you let an old friend say he's sorry he didn't keep his faith in you, Captain?"

Gentry's angry look softened. He took the hand, answered its firm grasp; and a smile came to his face. "Not Captain any longer, Sam."

"It may take only a day, or it may take a week. Or even a month," Grell said. "But I'll stake my commission on it being Captain again. And soon."

"And I'll stake mine." George Spires was shrugging into his coat and now he took his black bag from the table and came across to stand alongside Grell. "You'd like to be back with us, wouldn't you, Dan?"

Gentry thought about that deliberately. At length he looked up at Grell. "It's up to you, Sam. Keep Phil Fitzhugh strictly out of it and everything'll be all right. But if you don't, I wouldn't —"

"But I will, Dan. That's a promise. I'm getting busy on the wire the minute I get back up there."

Gentry was feeling a vast relief, not even minding the pain in his leg now. With a brief glance in Faith's direction, he asked, "Do I stay here?"

"You do," Spires told him. "I'll be down

to see you again around seven. We can try some hot compresses on your leg then. Meantime, shed your clothes and catch some sleep."

Gentry was still looking at Faith, and now she nodded, telling him, "Everything's arranged, Dan. Sarah's up the street right now telling Ralph he's to stay in the hotel tonight. She and I are sharing the front room."

"But —"

"No 'buts' about it, Dan," the medico interrupted severely. "The important thing is for you to get yourself mended. You can move out and into the room over Mike's office three or four days from now. But meantime you're to keep off that leg and give it a chance to heal."

Spires and Grell went to the door now, Grell lifting a hand to Gentry and smiling as he led the way out with Faith. And after Gentry had listened to the doctor giving Faith several parting instructions in the kitchen, then to the closing of the outside door, he eyed Clears to ask, "Can't you do anything about this, Mike?"

"Not a thing," Clears replied in mock soberness.

Gentry sighed and gave a slow shake of the head. Then he thought of something that made him ask abruptly, "What time is it?"

The saloonman took a watch from his vest

271

pocket and glanced at it. "Five-forty. Why?"

"No reason." Gentry was looking toward the window beyond Clears, noticing that the shadows along the alley were lengthening. Then his glance shuttled about the room until finally he found what he was looking for — his gun belt hanging from a nail almost out of sight on the wall behind the open kitchen door. The cedar handle of the .44 showed above the top of the holster.

Clears, watching him, asked, "What's on your mind?"

"Nothing," Gentry drawled, covering that untruth by asking querulously, "Why couldn't they let you haul me up to your place instead of strandin' me here with two women?"

Mike Clears grinned broadly. "From what I can make out, that won't be too hard for you to take." He came round from the foot of the bed now, chuckling at Gentry's embarrassed look. "Want some help getting out of your clothes?"

"No. I'll pull up a blanket and stay the way I am."

"The sawbones said to shed 'em."

Gentry shook his head. "That can wait till after he's been back tonight."

Clears shrugged and came over to unfold a blanket at the foot of the bed and spread it over Gentry. He went to the door then and paused there, looking around to say soberly, "I take it you're damned lucky to be here, friend. Sometime you'll have to tell me about it."

"I will, Mike."

The saloonman nodded and went out, closing the door softly. And afterward, for some minutes, Gentry lay there staring up at the new raw boards of the roof sheathing, his thoughts on something that kept him wide awake even though he was tired and his eyes heavy-lidded. He kept glancing impatiently toward the window, each time wondering why the light was fading so slowly against the oncoming dusk.

Abruptly he was startled at hearing a light tapping on his door. He called, "Come in, Faith," his soberness thawing as she opened the door and her slender shape stood there silhouetted by the stronger west light coming from the room beyond.

She came over to the bed and smiled at him. "You must be hungry, Dan. Can I bring you anything?"

"Later, maybe." A thought made him match her smile. "Now don't you wish you hadn't dragged me in here?"

A strange seriousness was in her then. "There's so little I've been able to do in all this, Dan," she murmured. "Don't try and

273

take it away from me."

He was noticing the way the light from the doorway outlined her head with a bright aura of spun gold and put her face in shadow so that it bore an even subtler delicacy than usual. Her beauty stirred him deeply. He knew his look must have betrayed the emotion in him when she said hurriedly, "I've been thinking of what you were trying to tell the captain about Ash, Dan."

"What about it?"

"You really do believe he'll be back, don't you?"

"I did. Now I'm not so sure," he lied. "Why?"

She ignored the question as she watched him closely. All at once she sank down onto the bed beside him. "If he took all those chances, he might still take another, mightn't he?" she asked.

She wanted an answer and he saw that he had to give her one. So he drawled, "As long as Caleb lives he'll take chances. But never foolish ones, Faith. He's too wise an owl for that."

"Would it be a foolish chance if he came back here tonight —"

Her glance was full on him, questioning, probing. That was his reason for saying very deliberately, "Look what he'd be up against.

The town warned against him, maybe a trap laid for him. No, he won't be back. I was wrong. Sam knew I was."

Her expression lost some of its gravity and he saw that he had almost convinced her. But then she surprised him by saying, "He must hate you, hate you bitterly. You're the one person who's stood in his way. He would kill you if he could." She turned and glanced toward the window, then faced him again to ask haltingly, "Would you mind if — could I just pull the blind down over the window?"

Gentry laughed softly. "Sure, pull it down."

The look she gave him then was humble, asking him to understand. And, seeing that his words might have offended, he put a hand on hers and said soberly, "Try to forget Ash, Faith. He's too busy saving his own hide to be thinking of making another try for mine."

She smiled relievedly, and her fingers closed about his briefly. Then she rose from the bed, went to the window, and drew the shade down all the way to the sill. Back beside the bed again, she told him, "You can get a good hour's rest before the doctor comes. And don't worry about using this room. The Blakes understand. They're both nice as can be."

He nodded, easing further down onto the pillow. She went to the door, pausing there to say, "That must have hurt terribly, his getting the bullet out. Is it better now —"

"Much."

"You'll call if you need anything?"

"Sure will."

She closed the door softly, and he listened to her steps fading out across the kitchen. For perhaps a minute he lay there wondering if he had really convinced her that her fear of Ash's coming down here tonight was groundless. He wasn't letting himself dwell upon the implication her worry had for him; something remained to be done before he could let himself weigh his feelings toward this girl or try and understand what she thought of him.

Now, quite suddenly, a strong impatience was in him as he glanced toward the window once more. He was relieved at seeing the strip of light along the blind's edge faded almost to darkness. Sight of that gave him a real sense of release, and at once he was pushing himself up and gingerly lifting his legs from under the blanket.

The dull ache along his thigh took on a harder pound which he tried to ignore. He bent his bad leg and, reaching down, tied the two ends of the cut denim about his calf to hold together the torn material. He sat a moment after he had lowered his legs to the floor, letting an unsettling dizziness drain away. And shortly he stood up off the bed and limped to the door. There, leaning against the wall and breathing heavily, he took down the shell belt and quickly buckled it about his waist.

He was pushing out from the wall again when he caught the slam of the kitchen door. Almost at once Sarah Blake's voice sounded in to him, and after several more seconds Faith's spoke in answer. As the two went on talking he crossed over to the bed, got down onto his knees and groped around beneath the bed. He found his boots there as he had hoped he would. Pulling them on quickly, he crawled on over to the window and came to a stand again. And now his forehead was beaded with perspiration, and the pain in his leg put a catch in his breathing.

He let the blind up with only a slight rustle of sound. The closed sash was stubborn, the unpainted new wood at first refusing to slide upward. When it did suddenly move, Gentry came rigid at the scraping sound it made. He hurriedly sat on the sill, ducked his head outside, and then, holding onto the sash, laboriously lifted his legs on out. Surprisingly little pain resulted from this maneuver, and as he slid gingerly down and caught his weight with his good leg against the ground outside he was feeling steadier than he had for some hours.

The shapes of buildings along the alley were already indistinct in the gathering darkness.

He was thankful for that as he hobbled down across the narrow yard to the gate in the picket fence. Twice when he hurried his bad leg caught his weight too abruptly, and a stab of pain shot into his hip. By the time he stood in the gate he realized he couldn't go on this way.

So he groped his way along the waist-high fence, feeling of each picket until finally he discovered a loose one. He pried it out from the others, jerked it loose. Using it as a cane, he tested it for a few steps.

Not bad, he told himself as he limped on. The leg complained only little more than it did when he stood still, although the constant throbbing above his knee increased steadily until he knew he would be forced to stop often and rest.

He made his first halt in the obscurity of a shed several doors below the *Lucky Find.* And as he leaned back against the shed's wall to rest, letting his heavy breathing subside, he suddenly thought about the Colt's being empty and lifted it from holster.

When it was loaded, the hammer resting on an empty chamber, he felt much better. He straightened again and hobbled on, wishing only that Ash's stable yard lay closer than the far end of the street.

Chapter Fifteen

Lamps were glowing in the cabins across the parade as Mary Fitzhugh came to the window of her bedroom, having just finished packing the top tray of her trunk. A faint stirring of the curtains before the gentle twilight breeze seemed quite in keeping with her thoughts. She felt almost at peace now, only one small doubt ruffling the surface of a beatitude that had been with her since midday.

She had today honorably acquitted herself in her obligations here. Proof of that had come late this morning there in the cemetery where she realized she had been the center of attention for officers and men alike. Not one of the troopers or civilians who had regarded her with such open respect and admiration — no, not even George Spires or Mike Clears — had known that her tears weren't being shed for Robert Fitzhugh, but rather in outright relief at her problem having so simply resolved itself.

She was free at last, free to go to Dan Gentry and humbly offer herself, offer to go with him to a new life remote from the grim and ghostly reminders of how weak and headstrong she had been. It still appalled her to look back upon her thoughts in that insane and brutal moment there in the cabin's other bedroom when she hadn't realized that the major lay there dead.

She thought back upon her conversation with Gentry there in the buggy behind the saloon the other rainy morning with much the same sense of shame. She hoped she hadn't offended him, hadn't said the wrong things about the Reed girl; it was jealousy alone that had made her try to turn Gentry against the woman.

But if she was halfway ashamed of the way she had acted, she was even more certain now that a few minutes with Gentry would settle their differences. What she was offering would make him forget her lapse. She had a supreme confidence in her ability to attract him, or any other man, physically. All she wanted now was the opportunity.

The packing of her belongings over the afternoon hours had been a necessary thing, a coming to grips with her new freedom. No one need ever know that she had ignored common decency to the point of being ready to leave here almost before the dirt had been smoothed over Fitzhugh's grave. She was taking no chances. Dan Gentry might be on the point of leaving, or taking the stage out tomorrow morning. If he did take it, she would be with him.

She wondered just now how she could explain a visit to the town tonight if anyone became curious. And, wondering, she happened to glance obliquely down this near side of the parade and made out George Spires's buggy standing before his quarters in the settling darkness. Not at all curious as to why the buggy was there, she thought only of how easy it would be to make the medico some excuse for wanting to borrow it.

She turned from the window, snatched her light coat from the bed, and was pulling it on as she went out and down the porch steps. But, a quarter-minute later, she was feeling a strong disappointment at seeing no light in the window of Spires's cabin. Even so, she went up onto the porch and knocked at his door. There was no answer.

She was standing there, eyeing the buggy and wondering what to do next, when she heard the solid crunch of boots approaching from farther along the path. Then shortly a man's shape moved in on her out of the gloom. She recognized Lieutenant Peebles.

"Good evening," she said as he came up on her. He saluted, and without waiting for his reply she asked, "Have you seen the doctor?"

Peebles glanced at the darkened cabin. "He's probably at Headquarters, ma'am."

"Perhaps." Mary was undecided for only a second. Then, her mind made up, she said, "Would you mind giving him a message for me, Lieutenant? I would like to go down to town to see the dressmaker." She was wondering as she worded the lie if she would ever again have to give this overworked excuse to anyone. "I know the doctor wouldn't mind my using his rig. But I'd like him to know where it's gone."

"You're going alone?" Peebles's concern showed strongly. "I should be honored if you'd let me accompany you."

"You'll do no such thing," she said quickly. "I'll be perfectly all right. The fact is, I rather enjoy the prospect. It's so long since I've been able to come and go as I pleased."

"Indeed it has," Peebles said respectfully. Then, moving over to the rig, he offered his hand.

Stepping up into the buggy she said, "Thank you, Lieutenant," in that low and purposely intimate tone she invariably used when alone with an attractive man. And again, as he unsnapped the tether weight from the horse's bit and came back to place it on the floor at her feet, she murmured, "Thank you. You are very kind."

The next moment she was regretting her coquettishness, for Peebles removed his hat to say haltingly, "I've been hoping you will — that you'll stay on with us for a time, Mrs. Fitzhugh. At least until the major's affairs are settled. Have you made any plans?"

"None as yet." Her tone had changed, taken on a brittle quality. She sensed at once a stiffening in him and hastened to add, "Though it's nice of you to be thinking of me, Lieutenant."

The smile she gave him as she lifted the reins and put the horse in motion left Peebles as he had been a moment ago, worshiping her charm and beauty. He saluted hastily, smartly, and she was very careful not to let her smile fade until the darkness hid him.

Never had she enjoyed the drive down along the rough bench road as she did this evening. The stars were brightening overhead, the cool breeze was like a tonic, and her thoughts were filled with longings and vividly imagined scenes of what it would be like once she and Gentry were together. She wasn't listening to the one small doubt that centered about the Reed girl. Instead, she thought of what an attractive couple she and Gentry would make. Walking the street of some city, Denver, perhaps, people would turn and look at them as she strode along with her arm through his.

She had a vision of being in Gentry's arms, whirling to the strains of a waltz across a polished ballroom floor reflecting the light of hundreds of candles glowing softly in crystal chandeliers. Her gown would be of pure white in contrast to her recent dress of severe mourning; it would accent her dark hair, and its cut would be subtly revealing. She had no illusions about her attractiveness, and it excited her to think of the countless ways she could make Gentry aware of her.

She had turned from the foot of the bench road and was walking Spires's horse up the alley before she quite realized she was in town. Idly, she happened to notice the new room on the back of the cabin surrounded by the white picket fence. This dwelling was the only one in town that made much pretense of being well cared for, and always as she came along the street she would notice it. Now she wondered vaguely whose it might be.

She had a bad moment as she drew in at the tie rail beyond the *Lucky Find*'s rear platform. What would Mike Clears think of her, coming here at night so furtively asking about Dan Gentry? But after a second or two's hesitation she stepped aground, hardly caring what he might think. She knew what she wanted, and none of these petty difficulties mattered any longer.

She knocked at the door almost timidly. Then, having had no answer, she rapped on the panel with all her strength. Abruptly the door swung open. An old, stooped man with a hawkish face stood there glaring out at her.

It was Ben Qualls and he began gruffly, "All you got to do is turn the knob and walk straight —" He saw who it was, surprise washing over his wrinkled face. "Oh, beg pardon, ma'am." And he opened the door wider.

Mary drew herself up stiffly and she entered the room holding her long sweeping skirt clear of the floor. She caught the taint of whisky and tobacco in the air and didn't like it; that showed in her crisp tones as she asked the oldster, "May I speak with Mr. Clears?"

"Not now, you can't." Qualls wasn't particularly impressed by her haughty manner. "He's down at Ralph Blake's waitin' for the doctor."

"Not Doctor Spires?" Mary was thinking of having taken the buggy when the medico might be wanting it.

"Ain't no other I know of."

Mary tried to ignore the ready sarcasm and even managed to smile. "Then would you happen to know Dan Gentry?"

"The captain? Sure do."

"Is he in town tonight?"

"Couldn't be much of any place else. Not with that leg."

Mary was puzzled, taking a moment to make any sense of what he had said. "His leg? What about it?"

Qualls forgot his testiness as he told her, "You must not've heard. Gentry stopped a bullet today. Crippled him bad, accordin' to what Mike said."

She caught her breath. Wide-eyed, she asked hollowly, "Where is he? Can you take me to him?"

The oldster shook his head. "Got to watch things here. But it's only down the street a ways. Ralph Blake's house. Know where it is?"

"No," Mary answered in a small voice, what she was imagining making her feel faint and deeply afraid.

Qualls tilted his head toward the alley. "Go back the way you come till you sight a white fence. That's Blake's. Maybe sixty or seventy yards below the —" He swore soundly then as the closing of the door interrupted him; for Mary hadn't waited to hear him out.

The moment she was on the buggy's seat once more she began sawing at the reins, trying to turn Spires's horse in this narrow space. She was frantic now, and when finally the scraping of the wheel rim against the box abruptly stopped and the buggy began rolling she reached for the whip and used it fiercely. Then almost at once she was having trouble pulling the animal down out of its run as the picket fence came up grayly out of the darkness.

She managed somehow to bring the horse to a stand before she had reached the end of the fence. Forgetting him then, she dropped the reins, jumped aground, and ran on in through the gate. There was a lighted window alongside the cabin's rear door. As she knocked she looked in and saw a stout woman slicing a potato into a frying-pan at a coal stove along the room's far wall. The woman only looked around, made no move to come across to the door; and in sudden anger Mary twisted the knob, pushed the door open, and started in.

She took one step only, then stopped. Faith Tipton stood there, had been about to open the door. It had nearly struck her as it swung so suddenly open. Now, as Faith saw who it was, her startlement gave way before a smile and she said graciously, "Do come in, Mrs. Fitzhugh."

Mary saw Mike Clears then as he came up out of a chair alongside a table to her right. And as the shock of finding Faith in the cabin, of understanding why she must be here, subsided, she ignored the girl and spoke to Clears. "I understand Dan's here. A man at your place told me he's been hurt."

Clears nodded politely. "Yes. But he's doing well enough."

His words dulled the apprehension in her. And then, still acutely aware of Faith, she asked, "Why didn't you let me know about this?"

Clears gave Faith a puzzled look. He shrugged, drawling, "No one thought of it, I reckon. Or maybe, we've been too busy lookin' after him since it happened."

Mary decided to overlook his mild reproach, not caring what he might be thinking as she asked, "May I see him?"

Again Clears's glance went to Faith, this time in a mute questioning. And it was Faith who said quietly, "Of course you may. He's asleep. But we're having to waken him for the doctor in a few minutes anyway."

She stepped on away from Mary now, leading the way to the bedroom door after taking the lamp from the table alongside Clears. It was galling to Mary to realize that Faith was so plainly in charge of the patient. Her anger must have been quite obvious then, for she noticed Clears turning away with a faint smile, and the other woman was staring at her in a way that only further provoked her.

Faith had opened the door and gone in through it. Mary, following, caught her choked outcry. The next instant Faith was calling in a small voice, "Mike, he's gone!"

Mary stopped just short of the door, Clears pushing hastily past her and on into the room. From where she stood Mary could see a rumpled blanket on the empty bed, could also see the open window beyond. And now Sarah Blake came over from the stove, looking in at Clears and Faith to ask solemnly, "How does it happen we didn't hear?"

Clears, coming out of the room hurriedly, shook his head in a baffled way. "Let's don't worry about how it happened. The thing now is to find him."

He took his hat from the back of the chair he had been sitting in. As he put it on he said brusquely, "If George arrives before I'm back tell him to stay right here. I'll get some help and we'll bring Dan to him."

He went to the outside door and hesitated there, looking at Faith who had come back into the kitchen. Seeing how pale she was, he said gently, "It's not your fault he's so bull-headed! Don't worry, nothing's happened to him."

He slammed the door heavily as he went out. Hardly had that sound died in the room's small confines before Mary, her eyes ablaze, was saying, "So this is the way you look after him!"

For a moment Faith's look was one of deep hurt. But then some thought brought a subtle change to her expression and more color came to her face. Then, paying Mary not the slightest attention, she came on across to set the lamp on the table. "Sarah," she said quietly, "I think I know where he may have gone. I'll get Mike and take him with me. Will you wait for the doctor?"

"Of course." Sarah Blake watched her go to the door. "You're not going without a coat! Take mine, you'll be cold."

But Faith only shook her head and went on. The door stayed ajar after she had gone, and for several moments both the other women stood listening to her quick steps fading out across the yard and up the alley.

Then Sarah Blake's voice abruptly cut across the stillness. "She'll find him."

Mary's blazing glance swung around on the woman. And Sarah, misreading it, said worriedly, "Here, honey, you sit down and rest, and I'll pour you some coffee."

Chapter Sixteen

The stable yard lay empty and shadowed. Only the faint pinkish glow of the forge's dying coals under the blacksmith's lean-to relieved the heavy obscurity. Along the back fence, the corral poles grayly streaked the blackness below the barn's hump-roofed shape. Now and then a horse's muffled hoof-thud would sound over the sibilant trickling of the feed-pipe at the log trough. The high-bodied shapes of two freight wagons rose over the low roof line of the ranked stables. Beyond them lay an open stretch, plain in the starlight. This wide wedge of the yard was what Gentry was watching.

He stood leaning in the open rear door of Ash's new building, the intended hardware store, knowing that he was well hidden in its black rectangle. He judged he had been here perhaps twenty minutes. Occasionally he would reach down and gently rub his thigh to ease its constant ache when it threatened to turn to numbness. This and the unwavering glance he fixed on the open stretch of the yard were the only two things that held his attention.

At first as he waited here he had thought about Ash, about the things the man stood guilty of. But in the end he had put from his mind everything but what he was sure was to come. Sometime tonight Ash would be here. He would be after a horse first of all. But Gentry was even more certain that the man would come to his shack just thirty feet away across the breadth of the gate.

The sounds echoing up from lower along the street were muted, seeming to heighten the stillness lying over the yard. It was perhaps because of them that Gentry's wariness didn't relax, so that when that whisper of sound, an alien note, shuttled faintly from the direction of the barn he caught it instantly.

It lacked completely any definition. He had almost decided that it meant nothing when abruptly and plainly he caught the low grating of wood scraping wood and knew that the gate of the corral was being opened. His glance went swiftly back there.

At first he could see nothing. Then suddenly Caleb Ash's big shape moved out of the obscurity. He was leading a saddle horse this way. Gentry reached down and drew the Colt's. But the next moment Ash swung in behind the nearest wagon and was gone.

For an interminable interval Gentry caught

no sound, saw nothing that let him know where Ash might be. Then all at once there was a movement at the limit of his vision. His glance whipped across to the shack. He was barely in time to see Ash's shape easing in through the door and out of sight. The man was taking no chances. He had stayed out of sight by walking the narrow passageway between the rear of the stables and the fence. He was moving soundlessly, like a shadow among shadows.

Gentry's first impulse was to wait right here. But then the speed with which Ash had moved from the rear of the nearest wagon shed and on into the shack warned him that when the man left there might be no more than two or three seconds in which to act. So at once he was reaching for the fence stake leaning against the wall behind him.

He eased on out of the doorway warily, putting his weight on the stake deliberately, carefully. When he was sure that his bad leg wouldn't buckle under him, he moved on. Only when he had gone several steps and was halfway to the shack did he realize that he was holding the Colt's in left hand, the stake in his right. But there was no other way he could walk; and, with thumb bent over the weapon's hammer, he went on.

He reached the corner of the shack, put his

shoulders to its back wall. The window's black rectangle was but an arm-reach away. Awkwardly, angling his makeshift crutch toward it, he took a short sideward step, then another.

Suddenly a flare of light wiped away the window's blackness. A match was burning in there. An instant later Gentry leaned over and was looking in at Ash kneeling on the floor by the bed. Alongside the man's knees was a board that had been lifted from the floor. And as Gentry watched, Ash bent over and reached deep into the opening where the board had been.

It was Gentry's intention to give the man a chance; he had never thought of anything else. So now, wanting to be sure of every move, he leaned the stake against the wall and took the Colt's in his right hand.

The thud of the stake falling to the ground behind him came like a gunshot. He had a blurred image of Ash straightening swiftly, of his dropping the match and his hand stabbing to the holster at his thigh. And as the room in there went suddenly dark, Gentry pushed himself out from the wall, wheeling back from the window.

He groaned softly as his bad leg gave way. He fell sprawling backward as the thunder of a shot from inside the shack blasted out the window. Glass shards sprayed his head and shoulders. A second shot came, the bullet ripping through the shack's thin wall, targeting the spot where he had been standing a second ago.

He lay there half stunned a moment. The next, Caleb Ash's massive bulk was wheeling fast out of the doorway. The violence of his sudden move lifted his left elbow from his side, and Gentry noticed that he had anchored that crippled arm at his belt, hand thrust inside his shirt.

A rosy stab of flame lanced from Ash's gun, lined at a spot waist-high along the shack's wall. That shot was thrown blindly at the point where Gentry had been standing alongside the window. The next instant he saw Gentry lying instead of standing; and his gun tilted downward.

Gentry caught that move as he threw the .44 into line. He was hardly aware of squeezing the trigger but saw Ash's high shape jarred backward at the bullet's impact. The man's weapon streaked flame again, lined upward now. He had barely caught his lurching balance when Gentry's second shot jolted him another backward step.

The rolling echoes of those explosions were slapping back from the canyon's near wall as Caleb Ash stumbled. With a broken, wheeling stagger, he fell heavily to the ground. A convulsive straightening rolled him onto his back.

Gentry was looking at the man across his sights, his finger tight to the trigger. Then Ash's shape went suddenly limp, and Gentry let his hand fall to the dust.

Deliberately, having to think out each move, Gentry got to his knees and crawled across there. He wrenched the Colt's from the man's clawed hand. The knowledge that Ash was dead left him abruptly weak and not wanting to move. He was straightening his bad leg, leaning to the side with his head hanging, when the first shouts sounded from down the street.

Faith and Mike Clears found him that way when they ran out of the yard door of Ash's new building several moments later. Clears had a gun in his hand. He was cursing profanely and with a pent-up fury as he followed Faith across to the two shapes huddled there behind the shack.

Faith came quickly to her knees alongside Gentry. "Dan!" she cried softly. "Are you all right?"

Gentry's head came up. He looked around wonderingly at her. And the slow smile that eased the bleakness from his lean face was very plain in the starlight. "Never better, Faith," he said. "Never."

Clears sighed gustily in relief and moved

around Gentry to peer down at Ash's massive, loose shape. Barely audibly, he breathed, "I hope to hell it hurt, really hurt!"

Then, hearing the pound of boots beyond the yard's slab wall as men ran in on the gate, he reached down to take Gentry by an arm and say urgently, "Better move on inside and let me keep this crowd from houndin' you, fella."

They helped Gentry to his feet and, each with an arm about his waist, were taking him in through the shack's doorway when the first trio of men pushed open the gates and bolted into the lot. Clears said, "You watch him, Faith," and turned quickly back out the door, slamming it behind him.

Gentry stood there in the blackness of the room, breathing heavily, hearing Clears call out to the newcomers. And now as he felt the pressure of Faith's arm leaving his waist, he caught her hand and held it, saying, "Don't go away."

Suddenly it seemed very necessary that he keep her here close to him. Her nearness was making him forget the complaint of his leg, the nightmare of that long wait out there in the darkness, what had happened afterward. And he had something to tell her.

"But you must sit down, Dan! Your leg must —"

The gentle pressure of his hand across her mouth cut short her words. And as his other arm went about her shoulders, turning her toward him, she seemed for the first time aware of the powerful emotion gripping him. He felt a tension leaving her, and a yielding to his embrace that awed him.

"Faith, what does a man do when he loves someone and has absolutely nothing to offer?" he asked humbly.

"Oh, Dan!" she breathed. "Dan, you're everything to me!"

He had his answer. He tilted her face up then and kissed her, kissed her tenderly, their embrace unlike that of the other night when they had been so swayed by that hunger for each other. Gentry was deaf to the sound of the many voices close outside, to everything but his awareness of the future's promise because of the trust this girl was putting in him.

Finally she put her head to his chest and he could feel her trembling. He ran his hand lightly over her hair, telling her, "You must be sure of this, Faith. We —"

The sudden opening of the door against his back cut him short. Faith still in his arms, he moved aside. Mike Clears stood there holding the door open a scant half-foot.

"Spires is here, Dan," Clears said. "Him

and Mrs. Fitzhugh. They both want to see you. How about a light?" He pushed the door wide then, wiping a match along its panel, adding, "There's a lamp across there on —"

He stopped speaking as he saw them standing there. An astonished, delighted grin came to his face. "I'm damned!" he said incredulously. "Wondered how long it would take you two to wise up to each other." His grin broadened, and he turned back to the door still holding the match, adding, "Just give a call when you're ready for the sawbones."

"Send him on in now," Gentry said.

He limped on over to the crate near Ash's rumpled bed and took the chimney from the lamp there, nodding down to it. Clears came across, struck another match and lit the wick. Then, pointing to the hole in the floor and the board lying near it, Gentry told him, "Reach in and see what you find, Mike. Ash was looking for something when I arrived."

He eased down onto the cot, and Faith came across to stand before him, both of them watching Clears as he went to his knees close by. And just then George Spires came in.

A smile akin to Clears's of a moment ago was wreathing the medico's narrow features as he eyed Gentry and Faith. "What was that I saw from out there?" he asked as he shut the door. Chuckling, he shook his head. "Mary Fitzhugh happened to see it, too. She'd been on her way in to you, Dan. That changed her mind. She's left."

Faith looked down at Gentry in a quizzical way that made him drawl, "Maybe she saw I was in good hands, George."

Just then Mike Clears said sharply, "Whoa! What's this?" He rocked back on his heels, a loose sheaf of papers in his hand. He eyed the topmost ones a moment and then held them out to Faith. "You may want these. That's your mother's writing, isn't it?"

Faith took the four small sheets, glanced at them, and nodded. Then George Spires was saying, "Better turn them over to Sam Grell. He's got orders to get what proof he can of everything Dan told us about Ash this evening."

"Proof?" Gentry asked. "Why? What're they after?"

Hesitantly, Spires answered, "I ought to wait and let Sam tell you himself, Dan."

"Tell me what?"

With a sigh, the medico said, "That you're ordered back to duty. That they're burning the records on your courts-martial and holding a new hearing."

Gentry's startled glance clung to Spires a brief moment before it lifted to Faith. He reached out and took her hand, trying to hide

300

his excitement, his eagerness, and delight as he solemnly asked, "How does that sound to you, Faith?"

"It's what you really want, isn't it, Dan?" When she saw the way his smile came, she added, "Yes, that's where we belong."

Peter Dawson is the *nom de plume* used by Jonathan Hurff Glidden for all of his fiction. It was also used once by Frederick Faust, better known as Max Brand, for a magazine story, and by Otis Gaylord for a series of eight novels. The name itself is derived from a popular brand of Scotch whiskey. Glidden was born in Kewanee, Illinois, and was graduated from the University of Illinois with a degree in English literature. He came first to write Western fiction because of prompting from his brother Frederick Dilley Glidden who wrote Western fiction under the pseudonym Luke Short. In his career as a Western writer, he has written sixteen Western novels and over 120 Western novelettes and short stories for the magazine market. Glidden from the beginning was a dedicated craftsman who revised and polished his fiction until it shone as a fine gem. His Peter Dawson novels are noted for their adept plotting, interesting and well developed characters, their authentically researched historical backgrounds, and his stylistic flair. His first novel THE CRIMSON HORSESHOE won the Dodd, Mead Prize as the best Western of the year 1941 and ran serially in Street and

Smith's WESTERN STORY MAGAZINE prior to book publication. During the Second World War, Glidden served with the U.S. Strategic and Tactical Air Force in the United Kingdom. Later in 1950 he served for a time as Assistant to Chief of Station in Germany. After the war, his novels were frequently serialized in THE SATURDAY EVENING POST. In paperback, his books have already sold 25,000,000 copies worldwide and have been translated into numerous foreign languages. Dawson titles such as HIGH COUNTRY, GUNSMOKE GRAZE, and ROYAL GORGE are generally conceded to be among his masterpieces although he was an extremely consistent writer and virtually all his fiction has retained its classic stature among readers of all generations. His short story "Long Gone" (1950) was adapted for the screen as FACE OF A FUGITIVE (Columbia, 1959) starring Fred MacMurray and James Coburn. His earlier classic Western novels are being reprinted in hardcover by Chivers, Ltd., for the English-reading world and many of his longer novel-length titles, beginning with RATTLESNAKE MESA, are appearing for the first time in book form.

The employees of THORNDIKE PRESS hope you have enjoyed this Large Print book. All our Large Print books are designed for easy reading — and they're made to last.

Other Thorndike Large Print books are available at your library, through selected bookstores, or directly from us. Suggestions for books you would like to see in Large Print are always welcome.

For more information about current and upcoming titles, please call or mail your name and address to:

THORNDIKE PRESS
PO Box 159
Thorndike, Maine 04986
800/223-6121
207/948-2962